I SPENT MY SUMMER VACATION KIDNAPPED INTO SPACE

**Other Apple paperbacks
you will enjoy:**

The Mall from Outer Space
  by Todd Stasser

The Computer That Said Steal Me
  by Elizabeth Levy

Help! I'm a Prisoner in the Library
  by Eth Clifford

Sixth Grade Secrets
  by Louis Sacher

I SPENT MY SUMMER VACATION KIDNAPPED INTO SPACE

Martyn N. Godfrey

AN
APPLE
PAPERBACK

SCHOLASTIC INC.
New York Toronto London Auckland Sydney

ISBN 0-590-43418-7

Copyright © 1990 by Martyn Godfrey.
All rights reserved. Published by Scholastic Inc. APPLE PAPERBACKS is a registered trademark of Scholastic Inc.

12 11 10 9 8 7 6 5 4 3 2   0 1 2 3 4 5/9

Printed in the U.S.A.   40
First Scholastic printing, June 1990

To Stephen, Wendy, Lisa, Melissa, Andy, Mike, Jeremy and Sarah with thanks for encouragement.

I SPENT MY SUMMER VACATION KIDNAPPED INTO SPACE

flushed the ion still from our engines. We were in
the process of leaving when your craft landed on
the asteroid. We couldn't pass up the chance."

"The chance of what?" Jared asked.

1.
Put Out Your Hands

Sometime in the near future . . .

I guess I should have protested more. I mean, if I'd *really* objected, we would never have been kidnapped by Torkan aliens.

But I let my best friend, Jared, talk me into borrowing a shuttle and flying offworld. We should have gone to the end-of-school party with the rest of the class. Instead, we headed for the asteroids.

I first met Jared on day one of sixth grade. We were in the same class at Bush Academy, just outside of Houston. Bush Academy is a private school for kids whose parents work for NASA-O, the organization in charge of sending settlers to new Outworlds.

When our alien physiology teacher told us to pick a lab partner, I headed straight for Jared. He was easily the most interesting-looking guy in the class. His sea-blue eyes and the way he tied

1

his long hair in a ponytail caught my attention right away. He sort of looks a little like me. I *knew* we were destined to become close friends.

"Hi," I said. "My name is Reeann. You want to be my partner?"

"I guess so." He didn't sound all that sure.

"Well, don't get too excited," I said sarcastically.

"It's just that I've never been partners with a girl before."

"So what?" I challenged. "Don't you like girls?"

"I like girls. I like girls a lot. In fact, if I hadn't been born a boy, I wouldn't mind being a girl myself."

It was so stupid, I had to laugh. That was the start of our friendship. And I suppose that if we hadn't been such good friends, I wouldn't have agreed to go offworld with him.

"Do you want to go to the party?" he asked.

"Sure," I replied. "Why?"

"Well, I don't think I really want to fly to that beach in Brazil. The teachers will only make us play games anyway. I'm not that excited about playing splatterball."

"What do you want to do instead?"

"I was thinking that we could sign out an Academy shuttle and go offworld. Go find an asteroid and look for bloodstone."

"Right." I laughed.

"I'm serious," he explained. "Doesn't the thought of zipping to an asteroid appeal to you more than a stupid old party?"

"We can't fly offworld by ourselves," I said. "You have to be thirteen to get your license."

"So what's a few months?" he reasoned. "Anyone can program a flight computer. A license isn't all that important. Besides, we won't go near a busy zone anyway. Nobody will see us."

"I don't know. We could get in trouble."

"Trust me." He grinned. "It'll be a great adventure."

Little did I know how true that statement would become.

"Well . . . ."

I should have protested more. But it did sound better than splatterball in Brazil. And Jared was right; nobody would find out.

So we signed out a two-seater from the Academy and I input a flight plan into the computer. As Jared said, there isn't that much to "driving" a shuttle. The computer handles everything from takeoff to landing. The driver just has to check that the instruments match the readouts. No big deal.

The shuttle lifted us out of the atmosphere at a gentle incline. We had to hold orbit for a few minutes before traffic control cleared us to the asteroids.

We spent the wait testing our geography knowledge as the earth turned below us. No matter how many times I go offworld, it always thrills me to see our planet from space. All that blue and white and soft purple gives me a neat feeling.

I've visited all the planets in the solar system and several Outworlds. It's great skipping the rings of Saturn. And the volcanos on Ohter, in the Beta Marcus System, are truly spectacular from orbit. But there's no place like home.

Being out there was scary and exciting at the same time. Frightening, because I usually traveled with my parents or my older sister, Leeann. Now it was me in control. And Jared, too, of course. But he's the same age as me. And exciting, because it made me feel grown-up. Sort of the same feeling I had when I first walked to school alone in kindergarten.

The shuttle pulled out of orbit and went pluslite as we passed Station Alpha. A few minutes later, we returned to true-time in the middle of the asteroids.

Traveling faster than the speed of light is not exactly my favorite sensation. I've read about the changes that happen to your body when you fly pluslite. Most of it I don't understand. What I do understand is how I feel. It makes me tingle — sort of an itchy feeling all over. Not only outside, but inside as well. It's like I've suddenly been plugged in. I'm always glad to return to true-time.

"Doesn't look like there's anyone else around," Jared observed.

"I'm not surprised," I said. "It's not the greatest place for a family picnic, is it? Can you imagine a parent suggesting, 'Why don't we have some fun? Let's go visit great hunks of nickel and iron floating in blackness.' "

"I'd go for that," Jared said. "I like the feeling I get in this place. It's like I'm the only living thing in the whole universe. It's being *alone*."

"Well, you're not alone," I pointed out. "I'm here. We're *alone together*."

"That doesn't make sense," he said. "How can we be *alone together*?"

Boys can be so dumb sometimes.

Jared pointed beyond the windshield. "Let's go bloodstone hunting on that one."

The computer identified the asteroid as F6HJ8, a medium-sizer, about one-and-a-half miles in length. The shuttle nosed right and eased to a landing on the sunside.

"Maybe we'll strike it lucky," Jared declared. "Go home with a bloodstone the size of your fist."

Bloodstone is a crimson quartz that's only found on the asteroids. It's worth a fortune on Earth, but the odds of finding the stuff are like those of winning the Pan-Galaxy Lottery. Even professional gem hunters don't bother looking for bloodstone. But there's always the hope that you'll trip over some. Stranger things have happened.

And stranger things were about to happen.

Once the landing pads were secure, we donned the ExtraVehicular — or EV — suits, decompressed the shuttle, and bounced onto the bleak surface.

A mile-and-a-half asteroid has so little gravity that if you make a slight jump you can find yourself flying into the great nothingness. With only two hours of air in an EV suit, that's not a healthy thing to do.

We shuffled along the surface searching for bloodstone pebbles. Nothing. After ten minutes, I stopped to look at Jupiter, about moon-sized from F6HJ8. The storm that has been raging for thousands of years in its liquid atmosphere was deep red today.

"You glad you came?" Jared asked through my earphones.

"Yeah," I told him. "This beats splatterball anytime."

"You got any plans for the summer, Reeann?"

"Not really," I said. "I'm going to Guide Camp on Mars for a week in July. And I'll have to visit my grandparents for a long weekend sometime in August."

"Where do they live?"

"Ganymede. You can see it from here. It's the

second moon on the right of Jupiter."

"I was there once. The whole moon is full of old people."

"That's because the atmosphere control makes it such a super place to retire," I said. "It's a perfect seventy-two degrees at every spot on the planet, day and night. And the gravity is less. That helps your heart and digestion."

"You sound like a travel ad," he chuckled.

"How about you? You still going with your mom when she visits the mining colonies on Como IV?"

"No," he said. "Her schedule was changed. She doesn't have to go till the fall. So I decided to stay home and do some extra studying. Our computer is on line with the Library of UGF now."

"You're going to do school stuff?"

"A little," he said. "I'm really worried about junior high. You know that I barely made it this year."

"So you'll be around Houston most of the time?" I asked.

"All the time."

"Except for Guide Camp and Ganymede, I'll be at home as well. You want to hang out together?"

"Course," he agreed. "Who else would I rather spend time . . . arrgh!"

"Arrgh!" I echoed.

Suddenly we were face-to-face with a pair of

Torkan aliens. They slithered from behind an outcrop and waved freeze pistols at us.

We stared at them, too stunned to do anything. What were Torkans doing on an asteroid in our solar system?

One of the Torkans began twirling the dial on his EV-suit radio trying to locate our frequency. The other continued to threaten us with his weapon.

Torkans are one of the fifty-six species that make up the United Galaxy Federation or UGF. We, that is us humans, were invited to join the UGF when we learned to fly pluslite and started visiting other stars, about a hundred and fifty years ago.

Torkans have been UGF members a lot longer than we have. In fact, they're one of the most common aliens in the Milky Way. They're also *humanoid* aliens. Humanoid is a term some long-dead scientist gave to aliens who have features similar to people. If an alien has two eyes, two arms, two legs, and a body, it's classed as a humanoid. No matter how different it is from people, it's still a humanoid.

Torkans have short, thick arms and legs. But their heads and bodies are huge — sort of like buckets on barrels. Also, they're completely covered with short gray fur. Our alien physiology teacher said that they look like ugly koala bears.

The ugly koala bear who was fiddling with the radio dial found our frequency. "Put out your hands," he barked in Unnerstan, the language used by most intelligent life-forms in the galaxy. "Put out your hands or you will die!"

2.
You Are Most Ugly

We raised our hands over our helmets.

"What's going on?" Jared asked. "What are you doing here?"

"Silence! I will ask the questions. What's going on? What are you doing here?" the dial fiddler demanded.

"Looking for bloodstone," I answered in Unnerstan.

The ugly koala bears began to babble to each other in Torkan.

Jared looked at me. "What do you think they're saying?" he asked in English.

"Silence!" the intercom crackled again. "Or you die."

I stared at the freeze pistols. There are worse things than being hit by a freeze ray, but not all that many. When a freeze ray hits you, it robs heat from your skin really quickly, like trying to hold onto a piece of dry ice. It takes the warmth so fast that it actually burns you. You end up with a ragged burn hole in your body.

They talked long enough for my arms to begin aching. Finally the dial fiddler addressed us again. "You will come with us," he said.

I guess the shock of meeting aliens in a place where there was supposed to be nothing but rock was starting to wear off. We didn't have to take this stuff. Torkans couldn't come into our solar system and behave this way.

"Now, just a minute," I protested. "You have no right to wave freeze pistols at us. And no right to order us around."

"You can't threaten to kill us," Jared agreed. "We have laws about that."

They started laughing in short barks.

"You will come with us," the other Torkan repeated.

"And what if we don't want to?" I sounded braver than I felt. "We're from Earth. We're citizens of the United Galaxy Federation, like you are. We're free to do what we want. What if we choose not to go with you?"

"Then I will blow a hole in your EV suit and you will explode," the dial fiddler explained.

"Oh," I said.

"That doesn't sound too pleasant," Jared said.

"You're going to be in big trouble when I tell my mom," I threatened. "She works for NASA-

11

O. When she finds out, she's going to be really upset."

Again they barked with laughter.

" 'When I tell my mom'?" Jared stared at me.

"It was worth a try," I said.

"Silence!"

The ugly koala bears escorted us across the barren surface of F6HJ8 until we passed into the darkside. Their spaceship was lit by two dim parking lights. We were pushed through the airlock, ordered to remove our EV suits, and directed down a narrow hallway. We entered a room furnished with two flight chairs. The chairs were equipped with magno-clamps.

"Sit down!"

We did as we were told. As soon as we were seated, the dial fiddler flipped the control and the magnetic fields pulled us heavily into the chairs. We were completely immobile.

The Torkans elbowed each other in a good-natured way. Dial Fiddler studied my face.

"You are most ugly," he grunted.

I watched his nostrils flare as he sucked air into his barrel chest.

"The feeling is mutual," I snarled.

"Bark, ha, bark, ha, bark, ha," he roared.

"What are you going to do with us?" Jared asked.

"We have plans," the other Torkan announced.

"For now, the only thing you need to know is that we want you to remain in these chairs until we return from the control room."

"We're not going to go anywhere in clamps," I pointed out.

Dial Fiddler nodded. "If you try to escape, you will die."

They turned, slapped each other on the shoulders, and left for the bridge. We could hear them laughing as they walked down the hallway.

I bent my head toward Jared — an uncomfortable thing to do in magno-clamps. "Well, you got any plans?"

"No," he answered.

"I figured you would be bursting with ideas," I said sarcastically. "I mean, it was your stupid idea to go bloodstone hunting on the asteroids. This is all your fault."

"You agreed," he said. "So it's your fault as well."

The fluxdrive engine began to vibrate. We felt the Torkan ship lift into space. I began to tingle as it went pluslite.

"Where do you think we're going?" I asked.

"Somewhere into space," he said.

"Brilliant. Why didn't I think of that?"

"I mean way out in space. Way, way out," Jared explained. "I have the feeling that those Torkans are not all that honest."

"What was your first clue?"

"I don't think they want to kill us," Jared went on. "If they did, they'd have done it back on the asteroid. As I said, these Torkans are probably outlaws. They've just committed a kidnapping. That's a capital offense in the United Galaxy Federation. That means we have to be way out in space, away from controlled territory. And, since we're still alive, we must be pretty valuable to them."

"Two whys," I said.

"No, I'm not too wise," he said modestly. "It's just logical."

"T-W-O W-H-Y-S," I corrected him.

"Right, I knew that."

"First why. Why were they on the asteroid?"

"I don't know."

"Second why then. Why kidnap us? Our parents aren't rich. The aliens don't even know us."

The speaker crackled to life. "Are you trying to escape?"

"No," Jared and I chorused.

"Good," the speaker said. "If you do, you will die."

"We get the message," I said.

The speaker crackled off.

It was Jared's turn to ask a question. "Do you think there's any chance the police will follow us?"

"I doubt it." I sighed. "We won't be reported

14

missing until night. They'll check with traffic control and send a search party. When they find our shuttle, they'll think we floated off and spend a few hours doing a sweep search. By that time, there won't be enough exhaust ions from the Torkan spaceship to detect, let alone follow."

"I was hoping you'd say something else. My dad is really going to be worried," he said dejectedly. "You know what he's like."

"Your father, my mother," I agreed.

A Torkan entered our room and gave us a suspicious stare. He'd changed from his EV suit into a loose-fitting robe, and I didn't know if he was the dial fiddler or the other one.

"I am going to release the magno-clamps," he told us. "We are light years from your home now. There is nowhere for you to escape. But if you try anything . . ."

". . . you will die," I finished.

The Torkan nodded and turned off the magnetic field. Being held by magno-clamps is a lot like having a shuttle parked on your entire body. When the field stops, the change in blood pressure makes you dizzy. That change, plus the tingling of warp speed, made me want to go to the bathroom. Desperately.

"I have to go to the bathroom," I told our captor.

"You wish to bathe?" the ugly koala bear asked.

"Not exactly," I said. "I have to use the facilities."

"The facilities?"

"The toilet," I said. "I've got to go to the toilet."

"Ah." The alien nodded. "It is behind the partition. Over there."

"Thank you." I eased out of the chair.

"If you try anything silly," the Torkan warned, "then you — "

"I know. I know," I interrupted.

Using a toilet designed for a giant koala bear is no easy task. I almost fell into the bowl, and the plumbing fixtures and hoses were all the wrong size, but a person has to adapt quickly in tough times.

When I returned, I found Jared in the middle of a conversation with our captor. It was obvious that Jared had asked my first *why*.

". . . finding you was a wonderful accident," the Torkan was explaining. "We'd outrun a UGF patrol and were hiding out in your system while we flushed the ion silt from our engines. We were in the process of leaving when your craft landed on the asteroid. We couldn't pass up the chance."

"The chance of what?" Jared asked.

"The chance of taking you," the Torkan said.

I asked the second *why*. "Why us?"

The alien scratched his furry ear. "My friend and I make a living dealing with . . . how shall I

16

explain this? . . . with exotic species. We deal in rare animals. Creatures that are on endangered lists. Or creatures that are declared too dangerous to remove from their home planets."

"But we're not exotic," Jared pointed out. "There are billions and billions of humans on Earth and the Outworlds."

"That is true," the Torkan agreed. "But where we are going you are very rare. Very rare indeed. And because of that reason, you will fetch a very rare price."

"Where's that?" I asked.

"Freetal," he said. "The main planet of the Freetal Empire."

Jared and I stared at each other in disbelief. The Freetal Empire was a group of twenty planets near the center of the Milky Way. They were well outside United Galaxy Federation territory. And they were definitely unfriendly.

The UGF once tried to begin trading with the Freetals, but we were rudely told to mind our own business. Their Emperor announced that anyone coming near his empire would be blown away. For safety reasons, citizens of the United Galaxy Federation are forbidden to have contact with the Freetals.

"But nobody is allowed to have anything to do with the Freetal Empire," Jared said.

"Really?" the Torkan arched his koala eyebrows. "I think you may be mistaken. In fact, I think the Freetals will be most happy to see us. I think they will find you a wonderful addition to their circus."

And with that, he started to bark-laugh again. "Yes, a wonderful addition."

3.
You Belong to the Circus

It took a good stan-minute for the Torkan's laughter to wind down.

"You hungry?" he asked as he wiped tears off his furry face.

"A little," Jared said. "You wouldn't have a Big Mac, would you?"

The Torkan shook his head. "We've got grub paste. In two flavors — natural and cooked."

"Natural grub paste?" Jared thought about that for a few moments. "I don't think I'm all that hungry after all."

The Torkan nodded and once again warned us how useless and fatal it would be to try to escape. Then he secured the door and returned to the bridge.

"We're in big trouble," I said. "We're going to Freetal."

"And we have to eat grub paste," Jared said.

"Freetal," I repeated. "That's over a hundred

thousand light-years from home. It's in forbidden territory."

"With no real food."

"Stop that. How can you be thinking about food when we're going to the Freetal Empire? Nobody is ever going to find us there."

"I'm not thinking of food, Reeann," Jared confessed. "I'm trying not to think about what you're saying. If I think about that, then I'm going to fall apart."

"This is a nightmare," I said.

"I can't even juggle."

I glared at him. "What are you talking about?"

"The circus. The Torkan said we were going to be sold to the circus. What good are we to a circus? Can you walk a high wire? Can you swing on a trapeze?"

"Of course not."

"You could be a clown," he suggested.

I growled at him.

"It wasn't really meant to be a joke, Reeann. I'm just scared. Honest. My head is sort of buzzing."

I sighed. "You know, I went to a circus at Disney World IX in Moscow once. They had an exhibit of unusual alien life-forms — the Weird Wonders of the Galaxy exhibit. Maybe that's why they want us. Maybe we'll be on display as weird wonders."

"That cheers me up," Jared said.

We spent the next few hours worrying. At first, we ranged through panic to just plain anxiety. After a while, a sort of numbness set in, and we tried to think of a plan to save ourselves. There was nothing we could do. The fact was we were prisoners, kidnapped into space, separated from our family, our friends, and our planet.

My body stopped tingling as we returned to true-time and the alien spaceship assumed orbit around Freetal, the head planet of the Freetal Empire and home of its antisocial Emperor.

The Torkans offered us another meal of grub paste before we were magno-clamped for landing. We refused. A few minutes after touchdown, our captors hustled us through the airlock and into the main terminal of the Freetal spaceport.

I'd been to the spaceport in Houston many times, so I was used to the bustle of a major terminal. And since Houston was an inter-planetary port, I was used to seeing aliens in all shapes and sizes. But I wasn't ready for the scene that greeted us.

The arrival area was a chaotic mess of thousands of creatures. Aliens of every description were speaking, barking, hissing, sucking, snorking, coughing, belching, grunting, and howling at each other. Half of them were the bald, wrinkled, humanoid, remarkably piglike Freetals. I could also identify several other species from alien physiology class, but many of them were new to my knowledge of life-forms.

"This is the only spaceport in the whole Empire that allows aliens to touchdown," one of the Torkans told us. "Their Emperor is suspicious of outsiders. But he realizes that it is sometimes profitable to trade with a few of us who can get him special merchandise, like you."

There were a good number of humanoids in different shapes and colors. In addition, I counted three Lizoids, including one legless snake lookalike. And I saw a few Quadroids, moving on their four legs, rudely snarling at anyone in their way. A couple of Insectoids scurried by and nervously clicked their mandibles. There was even a pair of chlorine-breathing Gortors carefully supporting their bulky helmets while waiting to clear security.

What really upset me about this crowd was the absence of any people. At Houston, most of the creatures in the spaceport were humans, like us. Here, Jared and I were the only ones.

This fact made us aware of just how far away from Earth we were.

"Can you believe this?" Jared muttered.

"You think I could vid-phone home?" I asked the Torkans.

"Silence!" they ordered together.

They hustled us through the crowd. Even in such a strange group, most of the aliens stopped what they were doing to curiously look at or sniff us as we passed by. One Insectoid stuck out its antennae and tried to examine us. Jared and I slapped the feelers away.

We stopped at a door covered with Freetal symbols that I couldn't understand. One of the Torkans pushed the handle and we entered a small room. It was quiet inside, a welcome relief from the noise of the spaceport.

The only furniture in the room was a compudesk. The creature behind the screen glanced up at us. To our surprise, Jared and I were looking at a human.

He rose slowly as if he didn't believe we were really there. Then he smiled at us, showing a row of brown, rotted teeth, and wrinkled, almost leathery skin.

"Well, I'll be a Gornese muck bug!" he exclaimed in English. "People. Honest to goodness, breathing, living humans. Real people. I never thought I'd see a real person ever again."

"Pleased to meet you." I extended my hand.

"And I'm pleased to make your acquaintance." The old man shook my hand. "I'm Gambini Pavolotti, but everybody used to call me Gam."

"Glad to meet you, Gam." Jared offered his

hand. "Can you get us back home?"

"Silence!" one of the Torkans commanded.

Gam scratched the gray stubble on his chin and regarded our captors. "Where'd you find these two?" he asked in Unnerstan.

"Matters not," the ugly koala bear told him. "They belong to us and we wish to sell them to the Imperial Circus."

"You scum!" Gam snarled. "You lowlife mud dogs. You can't sell these two. They're intelligent life-forms. They're citizens of the United Galaxy Federation. They've got laws against this."

"United Galaxy laws do not apply in Freetal Empire," the Torkan pointed out. "We wish to sell them."

Gam pounded his compu-desk. "They're children! They're youngsters."

"You tell them," I said. "Get them arrested."

Gam swore at the aliens in English and looked at us for a few moments before returning his attention to the Torkans.

"How much do you want?" he asked.

"You're going to buy us?" Jared gasped.

Gam ignored the comment. "How much?" he repeated.

The Torkan held up two furry fingers. "Two thousand Freetal Credits."

Gam shook his head. "Not worth it," he said. "Twelve hundred."

"Fifteen hundred," the Torkan said. "Having this species in the Imperial Circus will be a special treat. Your Emperor will be pleased. They are worth the price."

Again, Gam shook his head. "Look at them. They're skinny. And I bet they're diseased. Probably as sick as Burite sludge-suckers."

"They are healthy and strong," the ugly koala bear said. "They will put on a good show in the Circus. Fourteen hundred Credits."

"I'll give you thirteen. No more," Gam said sternly. "That's my offer. I ain't going to go any higher. Take it or get out."

The Torkans argued with each other and then handed our new owner a Galaxy Express charge card. Gam inserted the card in the desk, programmed the transfer of money, and handed the card back to the alien.

"You make me sick," he said.

"It's a living," the Torkan grunted. He nodded a good-bye to us, then he and his partner turned and left the room.

Gam bit his bottom lip. "Sorry," he muttered.

"What's going on?" I asked. "What's happening to us?"

"Do you own us now?" Jared wanted to know.

"I don't own you," Gam said. "The Emperor does. Or rather the Imperial Circus does."

"And you work for the Circus?" I asked.

"I don't really work for them. I'm the slave of the Circus Manager. She tells me to work as a buyer on this shift, and that's what I do."

"Are you going to help us?" Jared said.

"Like to. Sure would like to. Being that we're human and all that. But I can't. There isn't any way at all."

There had to be a way, I thought. Even if Gam was a slave on this crazy world, there had to be some way that he could help fellow human beings. After all, we'd been kidnapped and brought to this place. We were victims. Chromosomes were thicker than life fluid and all that.

"Could you turn your back while we walked out the door?" I suggested.

"I could do that," he agreed. "But it would be a mighty stupid move. I'd be dead by morning. I just paid thirteen hundred Freetal Credits for you. Anyway, it wouldn't do you any good. Do you think you'd be able to jump on the first space-ship home?"

"We could pretend to knock you out or something. That way you wouldn't be blamed for our escape," Jared said. "And we could smuggle aboard a transport back to the United Galaxy Federation territory."

"You're forgetting that the Freetals don't officially trade with us. Only outlaws and pirates come here, like those Torkans who kidnapped you.

Somehow, I can't picture you sneaking aboard one of their ships."

"It's worth a try though, isn't it?" I asked. "What other hope do we have?"

"None really. But like I said, if you escape, then I'm dead. So, I have an interest in making sure you stay here."

"Thanks a lot," I said.

"Now don't get angry with me. I'm a slave. I have no choice. And you belong to the Imperial Circus. You have no choice."

"We don't juggle," Jared said.

"Huh?" Gam arched an eyebrow.

"We don't have any skills that would be of any use to a circus," I explained.

"Oh." Gam nodded. "You've been thinking circus like on UGF worlds — clowns, wire-walkers, animals — that stuff."

"What other kind of circus is there?" I wondered.

Gam leaned back in his chair. He seemed reluctant to tell us. "You kids ever hear about an old civilization on Earth long before space travel? A thing called the Roman Empire?"

"Sure," I told him. "Named after the city Rome. What about it?"

"Well, the circus on Freetal is a lot like the circus in ancient Rome," Gam said.

"Oh, no," Jared gasped.

I looked at my friend. "Oh, no? What do you mean by 'Oh, no'? What's the big deal about that?"

"You don't know what they did in a Roman circus?" Jared's voice cracked as he spoke.

"No. So tell me. Why did you 'Oh, no'?"

Jared took a deep breath. "The Romans put people in an arena with wild animals like lions and bears. Then the animals would kill and eat the people for the pleasure of the audience. They called it a circus."

"Get serious," I scoffed. "They didn't do that."

"They sure did," Gam said.

I looked at him in disbelief. "Are you telling us that we were bought so that we can be eaten in front of a bunch of Freetals?"

He scratched his whiskers again. "I guess that's a pretty good description."

4.
To the Circus

"Now, I've got to finish my work," Gam told us. "Got a shipment of Horvian snow devils to take care of. But you can stay here in the office until I finish my shift, if you want to. It shouldn't take more than a few minutes."

"Where else can we go?" Jared asked.

"The holding pens. That's where the new Circus additions are supposed to wait. You might want to think about that, though. Those snow devils *do* smell a fair bit."

"We'll stay here," I said.

"It's more pleasant," Gam agreed. "And I'll take you to the Circus on the shuttle bus, if you promise not to do anything stupid."

"What's the alternative?" I wanted to know.

"You get shipped on the subway with the snow devils."

"We'll go with you," Jared said.

"Good. It's a little something I can do for you."

He pointed at a bench to the left of the door. "Have a seat."

The bench wasn't all that comfortable — it was designed for the short legs and wide rear ends of Freetals. But it seemed right that our physical discomfort matched our feelings.

"We're going to be eaten," I said to Jared.

"Don't say that, Reeann."

I pinched myself. "Look what I'm doing. I'm trying to pretend that I'm dreaming. I'm trying to wake myself up. Jared, this is crazy. This is absolutely, incredibly, completely, totally insane. Things like this don't happen in the twenty-third century."

He didn't say anything.

"Last week, I was worried that I was going to flunk my history test," I went on. "I couldn't remember the order of those old Presidents. Was it Jimmy Carter, Ronald Reagan, George Bush, Cher, or did Bush come before Reagan?"

"Cher was never President," Jared said.

"Yes, she was. I think. Maybe she was just Governor of something. Whatever, it doesn't seem so important all of a sudden."

I pointed at my chin. "You see this zit? When I got up this morning, I thought about making an appointment with the Avon Doctor to have it genetically removed. Can you think of anything so petty? One day, I'm worried about a zit, the next, I'm going to be eaten on the planet Freetal."

"Don't say that," Jared repeated. "Don't say anything, okay? I don't want to think about it."

So we sat in silence, watching Gam input the compu-desk. What was he doing here? How did a human end up a slave to the Imperial Circus Manager in the Freetal Empire?

He glanced at us once and smiled. I wondered why he hadn't been de-wrinkled. Why had his teeth gone rotten? He should have had them perma-capped when he was a kid. Surely he hadn't been a slave all his life.

"Well, that's it," Gam announced. "I told you it wouldn't take long."

He shut off the compu-desk and opened the door for us. "Let's go to the Circus. And remember, you promised, no stupid stuff."

Once again we moved through the busy terminal and took the escalator to the ground level. Things were only a little less chaotic there. Hundreds of aliens were pushing and jostling at the customs desks. The Freetal officials were snorting angrily at their visitors.

"Quiet night," Gam said as he waved an I.D. badge at an electric eye.

The door hissed open and allowed us to exit onto a transit platform.

"You must be pretty important," I said. "How come we didn't have to wait in line with everybody else?"

"I'm not important." Gam chuckled. "The Circus Manager sure is, though. Besides, I pre-cleared you through my desk."

It was a five-minute wait for the unirail bus. At one point, I noticed Jared looking at me with a raised eyebrow. It was his way of asking the question, "Should we try to escape?"

Our promise to the old man meant nothing. Why should we keep our word to someone who was escorting us to our death? But the realistic fact was that we had nowhere to run. Gam had been right; there wasn't any hope of smuggling ourselves aboard a spaceship. And where would we go in this alien city? We couldn't exactly fade into the background.

I shook my head at Jared, to tell him that we should play it cool. There might be a better chance to escape once we got to the Circus.

A bus packed with Freetals pulled up and we had to squeeze in before the doors closed. The pig-faced aliens grunted at each other, pointed at us, and studied us with their round black eyes.

"You get used to them staring," Gam said.

"We're not really going to have the chance to get used to anything, are we?" Jared grumbled.

"You could be riding with the snow devils," the old man reminded us.

The bus made frequent stops, and every time new passengers boarded there was a wave of excited snorting and sniffing.

"Kind of funny language, isn't it?" Gam said.

"How do you say, 'Move your bacon'?" Jared asked.

The old man looked at my friend as if he didn't understand what he was talking about.

A half stan-hour later, Gam directed us from the bus onto an empty platform. "This is the stop for the Imperial Circus," he told us. "There ain't nobody here now, but come tomorrow, the place will be crawling — thousands of them coming . . ."

". . . to see us eaten," I finished.

Our footsteps echoed off the concrete as we passed through a large doorway. We were met by two Freetals dressed in blue overalls.

"These are your keepers," Gam said. "Be good or else they get sort of nasty. Remember they're used to taking care of more dangerous species."

The Freetals examined us and made a couple of pleased grunts. One of them reached out and squeezed my arm. I snarled and pulled it away.

"Look," Gam said. "I've got to go now, but I just want to say . . ." He paused as if he were searching for the right words. "Well, things ain't exactly as they seem. I like what I've seen in the last hour. You may be just what we're looking for. I've got to go make a report, and if I can get through to the Emperor's office, then I may be able to do something about your problem."

"The Emperor?" Jared and I said together.

"The leader of the Freetal Empire," Gam said. Then he paused again. "I'm telling you too much already. I can't promise nothing, but I'll try. I'm sure going to try. The more I think about it, the more perfect you seem for the part."

"What part?" I asked.

"No, I can't say nothing. I've probably told you too much. Let's just leave it at the point where I'm going to try."

"Whatever you do, we'll appreciate it," I said hopefully.

"Right." He nodded. Then he walked back out to the platform.

"What do you make of that?" I asked Jared. "First, he tells us there's nothing he can do. Then he says he's going to talk to the Emperor of this place. Since when does a slave talk to an emperor?"

"Weird," Jared agreed.

"Come with us," one of our new captors commanded. "If you try to escape, you will die."

Jared and I gave each other a knowing look and

let our keepers guide us through a maze of hallways.

"You know," I said to my friend, "I think the first thing that an alien learns in Unnerstan is how to threaten someone with death."

"Silence!" a Freetal guard ordered in Unnerstan. "No strange babbling. If you are not quiet, you will die."

We did as we were told.

Our room was a little larger than a closet. There was a small toilet behind a screen, but no beds, chairs, tables, or anything else. There wasn't even a door. As soon as we entered, a clear orange force field crackled across the doorway.

And every two stan-minutes, one of the guards would walk by and peer through the force field to make sure that we weren't trying to escape. Maybe they expected us to eat a hole in the wall.

Jared and I sat on the floor, leaning against opposite walls. For a long time, we didn't say anything.

"You know, Reeann?" Jared broke the silence. "I'm really scared."

"Me, too," I said. "I keep thinking about tomorrow."

"Can I tell you something that I've never told anybody else in the world?" He looked around our cell. "That I've never told anybody else in the whole galaxy?"

"Sure."

"I want to tell you about my blankie."

"Your what?"

"My blankie."

"Your blankie?"

"Don't look at me like I've blown a baffle," he said. "My blankie. I know it sounds dumb, but it's important to me."

"Your blankie?"

"When I was a baby I had this little yellow blanket. I took it everywhere. I didn't feel right without it. You ever have something like that?"

"I had a plush poodle when I was small," I said. "It was my favorite toy."

"This blanket wasn't a toy. It made me feel safe whenever I went outside. I used to scratch it and I'd feel better. Anyway, I couldn't say 'blanket.' The closest I could get was 'blankie.' Stupid, huh?"

"My baby word for 'juice' was 'duce,' " I said.

Jared crossed his fingers. "Me and that blanket were this close. Even when I got older, I wouldn't let my parents throw it out. Even when it was in pieces."

"My plush poodle fell apart."

"So did my blanket. By the time I started play-school the only piece left was this big." He held up his hand. "I kept it in my pocket."

"Little kids are weird," I said.

"You want to hear something stupid? I still have that piece of baby blanket. In kindergarten, I realized that if I didn't do something, my blankie was going to become extinct. So I tucked that little yellow scrap at the very back of my underwear drawer to be used in case of emergency."

A tear rolled from his left eye and trickled down his cheek.

"An emergency was a civics test. Or my public speech. I used to pull out my blankie, give it a few scratches, and I'd feel better. I wish I could do that now."

He wiped the wetness from his cheeks. "You must think I'm a real wimp. Here I am, almost in junior high, and I'm thinking about a stupid security blanket half a galaxy away."

I shook my head. "When you think about where we are and what's going to happen in the morning, you're acting really brave."

He sniffed back another tear. "Thanks, Reeann. You're being really brave as well."

"I don't feel it," I said. "When I get worried or upset about something, I ask my mom for a hug. That helps me. Would you think I was being a wimp if I asked you for a hug?"

It was my turn to cry. My fear moved through my insides and seemed to explode behind my eyes. All of a sudden, hot tears flowed down my face.

I watched a blurry Jared crawl across the floor and felt his arm around my shoulder. He pulled me close.

"It's going to be all right," he said. "We'll think of something."

"We'll think of something," I echoed.

But what?

5.
The Real Problem

The Freetals offered us a bowl of lumps for supper. It smelled like scrambled eggs and old cheese, but tasted like warm, salty yogurt.

"What do you think it is?" Jared poked at it.

"Grub paste?" I said.

Whatever it was, we were both so hungry that we ate it all. Despite the salty aftertaste, a full stomach seemed to take the edge off my fear, and when I stretched out on the dirty floor it took only minutes to fall asleep.

The next thing I knew someone was shaking my shoulder.

"Come on," Gam coaxed. "Wake up."

I rubbed my eyes and temples. For a moment, I was confused. What was an old man doing in my house? And why was I on a dirty floor? Then the reality of the Freetal Imperial Circus washed over me.

"It's morning," Gam said as he began to shake Jared. "Wake up, boy."

"I feel so heavy," I mumbled.

"They put something in the food so you'd fall asleep," Gam told me. "Just to make sure you're not a problem. And to make sure you're in good shape for the games."

"Good shape to be eaten," moaned Jared as he sat up. He looked as foggy as I felt. "I've still got the salty taste in my mouth."

There was a small tray near the now de-charged doorway. Gam grabbed the two mugs from the tray and handed them to us. The cup held a syrupy, hot liquid.

"This is what the Freetals drink for breakfast. It's the closest thing to coffee," he explained. "Drink up. I've got to talk to you."

I took a couple of sips, enjoying the sweet taste, and felt the fog slowly clear.

"Listen up," the old man began. "I sent a report to the Department last night and got you approved."

"What's that mean?" I asked.

"It means I can get you out of here, if —"

"All right!" Jared exclaimed.

Gam shook his head. "I said *if*. I can get you out of here *if* I can get the Emperor to approve my plan."

"Will that be a problem?" Jared asked.

"He'll agree when I get to talk to him," Gam told us. "But that's the real problem. To get the ear of the Emperor, you have to go through the right channels. You have to go through a sub-minister, an assistant minister, a deputy minister, the Minister herself, and only then do you get the Emperor's attention. It's the system, so to speak. Even someone like me can't shorten the time it — "

He stopped as if he were telling us something we weren't supposed to hear.

"Why would the Emperor listen to you?" I asked. "You're a slave. You're a human like us. Our species gets sold to the Circus. How come you can get the Emperor's attention? And what do you mean about the Department? And what's *your* plan?"

"You ask too many questions, girl." Gam seemed angry. Then he sighed and bit his bottom lip. "Look, I can't tell you everything right now."

"When do you think you'll get to speak to the Emperor about us?" Jared asked.

"It could take hours," Gam grumbled. "And that's a major problem right now. You see, you've been moved up on the program. You're now the opening act. We're going to be awful close."

"Can't you change the Circus schedule?" Jared suggested.

Gam shook his head. "You are owned by the Circus. You're going to be on vid all over the planet. The only one who can stop it is the Emperor. If only I'd thought it out a little more, given myself more time."

"What are you talking about?" I asked.

"Later," he said. "Right now, I want to tell you to try to stay alive as long as possible. When they throw you into the arena with those Andovian slime worms, try to stay out of their way. Don't give in. We might get the OK from the Emperor's office while you're out there."

"Slime worms?" I gulped. "You mean we're being thrown into an arena with Andovian slime worms?"

"That's right," Gam said.

"Holy moly." Jared looked at me.

"Yeah, holy moly," I agreed.

"That's why I wanted to tell you to stay away," Gam explained. "Lots of creatures see those worms and just give up, roll over, and wait to die."

"Slime worms," I muttered.

The old man patted me on the shoulder. "Just stay away as long as possible."

Then he walked out of our room. The orange shield crackled on as he left.

"We don't stand a chance against Andovian slime worms," I moaned. "What are we going to do? And how come you look like that? How come you don't look scared? Didn't you just hear what Gam said? We're going to be eaten by Andovian slime worms. How come you're acting so calm? How come . . . ?"

Jared held up his hand to stop me. "I think I may have an idea. What do you know about slime worms?"

"What kind of stupid question is that? I know they're huge and they have big teeth."

"What do you know about them scientifically? Tell me what you know," he asked.

"This is a strange time to play trivia games," I said.

"Tell me."

"Okay, but I feel really stupid. Slime worms get their name because their bodies are covered with a slimy, mucus liquid. This liquid protects their sensitive skins, turns off predators, and helps them move. They slide about on a layer of the stuff. Most slime worms are smaller than your hand. A few are as big as snakes, and there's one giant species, the fifteen-foot-long Andovian. Most eat plants; the Andovian eats meat. It's going to eat us. Is that what you wanted to hear?"

"Maybe," Jared said as if he were concentrating on something else. "Do we have any slime worms on Earth?"

"Yeah," I said. "We call them slugs."

Jared slapped his hands together. "That's what I thought. The salty food gives me an idea. I remember when we had slugs in our garden. My

43

mother killed them by throwing salt over them."

"So?"

"So." He grinned. "That's how we're going to beat those Andovian slugs."

"We're going to beat Andovian slime worms by throwing salt on them?"

"A great idea, huh?"

I looked around the room. "I don't see a salt-shaker. And I don't see how that would help us, anyway. How are we going to get enough salt to slow down fifteen-foot monsters?"

He thought about that. "We don't need all that much. Just enough to throw at their eyes. Enough to make them lose interest in us."

"So we still have the problem of how we're going to get the salt in the first place. We can't go to a 7-Eleven, can we?"

"Think then," he said. "There's got to be a way."

We sat in silence for a minute, maybe more.

"Anything?" he asked.

"Well, it may be a long shot but . . ." It didn't take me long to explain the details of my plan.

"It'll never work," he told me when I was finished. "The guards won't believe it."

"Why not?" I said. "Outside of Gam, they've probably never seen a human before. They have no way to know we're not telling the truth."

"I don't know. . . ."

"It'll work," I said. "As long as you act better

than you did in the Christmas play."

"What do you mean by that?" Jared looked offended. "I was a great Ghost of Christmas Past."

"You kept forgetting your lines."

"Scrooge gave me the wrong cues," he said.

"Let's not argue about it. If you're right about the salt then this is our best, maybe our *only* chance. You got a better idea?"

He shook his head. "No, let's go for it."

6.
Salt Eaters

Jared lay on the floor with his knees pulled against his chest. I stood by the force field.

"You ready?" I asked.

"All set," he answered. Then he began to groan. "Aaarrrggghhh! Ooorrrggghhh!"

"Don't overdo it," I whispered. "You have to sound realistic."

"You do your part and I'll do mine," he whispered back.

"Make it better than the Christmas play," I said.

"Eeerrrggghhh!" Jared moaned again.

I turned around. "Help!" I shouted through the charged doorway. "Please. Help!"

Instantly a keeper appeared. He defused the screen and waved a freeze pistol to force me to back away. Then he glanced at Jared.

Jared held his stomach and continued to make loud, gutful moans.

"Aaarrrggghhh!"

"What's wrong with him?" the guard demanded. "Why is he making that noise?"

I tried to put total panic into each syllable. "He's dying. It's salt shock."

"What?" the Freetal asked.

"Ooorrrggghhh!"

"Salt shock," I explained. "Your food isn't salty enough. We need lots of salt in our diet." I cupped my hands together. "If we don't get this much salt, we go into shock and die."

"Uuurrrggghhh!"

Don't overact, I thought.

The keeper eyed Jared suspiciously and then thrust the freeze pistol into my face. "Is this a trick? Are you trying to escape?"

"Please help him," I pleaded. "Get us the salt. If you don't, then he'll be dead before the circus starts."

"Iiirrrggghhh!"

Still pointing the weapon in my direction, the guard bent over to take a closer look at Jared.

Come on, pig face, I thought. *Go get some salt.*

"He's going to die!" I repeated.

Another keeper appeared in the doorway. The guard inside the room grunted to him in Freetal language, and the second guard vanished down the hallway.

"He will bring salt," I was told.

While we waited, Jared continued to groan on

the floor. He added a few rolls and jerks for effect.

A stan-minute later, the second guard reappeared with a clear plastic bag. There had to be a pound of salt inside. The keeper with the pistol took it and then handed it to me.

"Is this enough?" he asked.

"I think so," I said.

"Then fix him. Fix him so that he doesn't die."

I bent over Jared with my back to the guards. I pretended to pour salt into his mouth. Jared stopped moaning and thrashing, but stayed on the floor. He winked at me as I stood up.

"He'll be fine now," I announced. "But we have to keep the salt. We'll need it later."

The first guard scratched his chin with his free hand as he thought about my request. "How come you do not have this salt shock? Are you not hungry for salt as well?"

"Oh, yes," I told him. "I'm starved for salt."

"Then eat some," he ordered. "I want to see you eat the salt."

"You want to see . . . ? Okay, no problem. I'm really salt hungry." I reached into the bag, grabbed a handful, and began to lick it out of my palm.

Immediately my cheeks and tongue began to burn. My mouth filled with salty spit, and I had to fight the urge to gag.

"That is pleasant for you?" the guard asked.

I felt sweat break out on my upper lip and nose. I made a hideous smile at him. "Tast's gre't," I slurred through the stinging mass in my mouth.

"Then they should call you Salt Eaters," the guard said. "Perhaps you will be too salty for a slime worm to eat."

The guard by the door started laughing at that comment.

Tears were streaming off my chin. I swallowed a mouthful of salty spit, and my stomach protested with a dry heave.

"Enjoy your salt," the first guard said as he ushered his fellow Freetal into the hall. As soon as the force field recharged, I dove behind the screen and horked the wet salty ball from my mouth.

"You okay?" Jared called.

"Wundurful," I replied. "Jus' wundurful."

I wiped my lips on my sleeve and returned to the room. Jared was sitting up, leaning against the wall.

"I'm a great actor, huh?" he bragged.

We said very little to each other while we waited for the Imperial Circus to begin. There wasn't anything to talk about. The hundreds of things that seemed to interest us on Earth — school,

friends, holopics, the vids, music, whatever —
meant nothing anymore. In a short time, we were
going to face Andovian slime worms and try to
stay alive.

I tried not to think about what was going to
happen, but a picture from my grade five science
text was stuck in my mind. It was a photo of an
Andovian slug with its head raised to attack a
small deerlike animal. The little animal was par-
alyzed with fear. Its eyes were staring into the
slimer's pizza-sized mouth, transfixed on the circle
of carving-knife teeth. I kept seeing that picture — only it was *me* looking into the slime
worm's mouth.

I wondered if Gam would return to tell us that
the Emperor had freed us from his Circus, but
the only creatures who moved on the other side
of the force field were our keepers.

I didn't really expect Gam to save us. He was
a slave. How could he speak to the Emperor? And
what was all the talk about Jared and me being
approved? And his *Department*? I suspected that
our fellow human wasn't all together in the head.
Maybe being stuck on Freetal had messed up his
thinking. I could see how that could happen.

Jared was deep in his thoughts, focusing on the
wall behind my head. Every few minutes, he
would pat the salt in his pockets as if it gave him

strength to know that it was still there. Maybe the salt was a blankie substitute. Despite my bulging pockets, I didn't feel an equal to a flesh-eating slug.

And then it was our time. . . .

The keepers pulled us to our feet and, waving freeze pistols at our heads, directed us through the maze of hallways. We came to a staircase and climbed to a large, empty room. A Freetal wearing a long white robe met us.

"I am the Circus Manager." She introduced herself in Unnerstan. "Welcome to the Imperial Circus."

What did she want us to say? *Thank you?*

We didn't reply.

"I am told that you speak," she went on. "My keepers say you are an intelligent species. It is unusual to have an intelligent species compete in our circus. We usually choose our entertainers because of their special savage skills. It will be refreshing to have an intelligent creature in the arena. You will give us a good show."

She seemed to wait for us to make a comment, but we remained silent.

"Do you understand what is about to happen to you?" she asked.

We didn't answer.

"Yes, you do." She smiled. "I can tell that you

know. I can see the fear in your eyes."

I wondered what would happen if I took a swing at her piggy face.

"You should consider this a great honor," the Circus Manager continued. "To die for our entertainment is truly a noble cause. You should be delighted to end your life in such a dignified way. Although the Emperor is not in the audience today, you can be assured that he will watch your deaths on replay. You should take great pleasure from that fact."

Again, she waited for us to speak.

"Nothing to say to me? Perhaps, you would like to say something that I can record in the Circus records. As I told you, having an intelligent species is a treat for us. Perhaps you'd like to tell us how it feels to know that you will soon face the giant worms."

Silence.

"No last words?" she coaxed.

"Eating carrots makes your hair curly," Jared said.

"What?" the Manager wondered.

"The moon in June is a big balloon," I added quickly.

"What is this?!" she demanded.

"Peter Piper picked a peck of pickled peppers," Jared went on.

"Little Miss Muffet sat on a tuffet," I told her.

52

The Manager took a step backward. "You are not intelligent. You are insane."

"Salt Eaters," one of the guards volunteered.

"Prepare to die!" She almost shouted the words at us.

The keepers scrambled behind her as she stomped out the doorway and down the staircase. As soon as the Freetals left, a real, very solid door slid across to block the exit.

"Great last words," I said.

"Yours were pretty good, too," Jared praised. "There was no way I was going to give that porker any jollies. I could tell that she was just waiting for us to beg for mercy or to get angry. She was enjoying herself." Then he patted his pockets. "Instead, we'll give her a little surprise."

I wished I shared his confidence.

There was a loud, mechanical noise, like huge gears grating against each other.

"This is it," Jared whispered.

Slowly the opposite wall began to rise toward the ceiling.

7.
The Big One Is Yours

As soon as the far wall disappeared into the ceiling, the wall behind us began to edge forward, forcing us to move with it. It stopped flush with the vanished wall.

Jared and I stood on the floor of a square arena. Each side was about half as long as a football field. A wall as tall as a basketball hoop surrounded it. The wall and floor were made of the same cementlike material.

Around the outside of the arena was the audience — a mass of Freetals stretching a hundred rows to a domed ceiling. When we emerged, they began cheering.

In such a large group, they looked even more piglike — a crowd of Porky Pigs. Several of them waved and shouted at us in their language.

Then twenty thousand Freetals turned in unison to stare at the far wall of the arena. A section of the wall moved upward revealing another hid-

54

den room. Two brown, green, and gray slime worms crawled into the arena. This cranked up the volume of the cheers.

Seeing a picture of an Andovian had in no way prepared me for the real thing. Two whale-sized monsters of muscle and slime oozed across the arena floor. One was slightly bigger than the other, but they were both hideous giants compared to us.

"They're real big," I said.

"We've got salt." Jared tried to reassure me.

The worms slid away from their wall, leaving a trail of glistening mucus. They lifted their tubular heads and made wide circles in the air with their long antennae as they searched for scents.

Their sickening silver-gray underbellies were patterned with two rows of black slime glands. The glands joined just below their circular mouths. I stared at the teeth beyond the blubbery lips.

"We've got salt," Jared repeated in a less confident voice.

I held the momentary hope that the crowd of Freetals would confuse the antennae of the Andovians. Perhaps they wouldn't be able to find us with an arena full of aliens smelling up the air.

No such luck. Both worms pointed their antennae in our direction, dropped back onto their bellies, and slid toward us.

Jared pushed my shoulder and we moved to the right. The worms adjusted their path to match ours, and the crowd began to hoot wildly.

We turned the corner, and the large worm broke at an angle. It crawled directly to the place where we were headed. If we continued to go right, they'd have us trapped.

"Run between them!" I shouted.

Jared nodded and grabbed my hand. We darted between the monsters, running so fast that we almost bounced headfirst off the other wall. The worms circled in confusion, trying to pick up our scent.

The Freetals began to stomp their feet and make an uncomfortable, high-pitched whistling sound. I think it was a sign of approval.

The worms located us and twisted around. Rapid contractions of their slimy bodies closed the distance.

"Let's try left this time," Jared suggested. "But let's move faster."

We jogged along the wall and turned the corner. The worms, obviously frustrated that we weren't an easy meal, began to hiss. The audience loved this added extra and stomped its collective feet more urgently.

We had worked ourselves to the other side of the arena — the wall where the slimers had appeared. The creatures were turning slowly, moving toward our new location. I figured we were in good shape. If we kept moving, we should be able to keep the Andovians a fair distance away. We could play tag and they'd always be It. That's what I thought. . . .

That great plan fell apart when I fell flat on my rear end. An instant later, Jared slipped beside me. We had tripped in their mucus trails.

I frantically tried to regain my footing and stumbled onto my knees. My shoes, clothes, and hands were soaked in the thick saliva-like fluid. It was as if I'd been smeared with grease. I tried to stand again and slid sideways.

The crowd turned its cheering up a few decibels more when it saw our problem. The worms were slithering closer.

Jared managed to wobble away from the guck. He grabbed my arm with his slimy hands and steadied me as I stood up.

"Run!" he shouted.

We tried, but lost our balance and slipped back into the ooze.

The crowd noise became deafening.

Jared leaned over to yell into my ear, "Time to fight back!"

Using each other for support, we regained our footing. Jared wiped his hands on the front of his shirt in an attempt to remove the goo. Then he reached into his pocket for a handful of salt.

Again, he leaned over to shout at me. "The big one is yours!"

"What?!"

He didn't hear me. My voice was lost under the cheers and hoots from the Freetals. Not that it was our decision, anyway. The larger one had obviously chosen me. The Andovian raised its head, exposed a gaping mouth, and slimed in for the first taste of its dinner.

I wiped my hands on my jeans, grabbed for the salt, and raised my arm, ready to throw a fastball of salt right into the monster's face. The slime worm tipped its head a little further and then lunged at me.

As I brought my arm around, my feet flew out from beneath me, and I fell heavily to the floor. Fortunately the Andovian was as surprised by this as I was. Its teeth snapped at empty air.

Lying sideways in the mucus trail, in the shadow of the beast, I completed my pitch. The salt flew in a cloudy ball and stuck to the creature's underbelly. Immediately the salt-covered skin began to bubble.

Fumbling to my knees, I grabbed another fistful of salt from my pocket. The slimer was now flat and I had a perfect shot at its antennae and tiny black eyes. My aim wasn't perfect, but I scored a cloud of salt in one eye. Large, clear bubbles foamed on the skin.

The monster recoiled and released a horrible hissing screech. I took the opportunity to roll out of the mucus trail onto dry floor.

The worm was whipping its head back and forth, obviously in distress. I stood up and scraped the bottom of my shoes on the cement to remove as much gunk as possible. Then I inched forward to throw another pitch at the worm's side. When this volley hit and the bubbles began, the slimer jerked. It twirled, wrapping itself into a tight knot and then stretched straight out. It hissed in anger and pain.

The skin that had been hit by the salt turned from brown and gray to a milky white.

I stared at the Andovian for a few moments, fascinated by its contortions and heaving, before it hit me that somewhere in this arena, my best friend was also fighting for his life.

I turned around and found Jared standing behind me watching the retreat of my worm.

"Nice work," he grinned.

"You okay?" I asked.

He nodded. "My first handful hit it in the eyes. It just turned and ran — so to speak."

He pointed to his left, and I saw the other worm moving away from us, its whole bulk shaking in painful spasms.

I returned his grin, and we gave each other a salty, sticky high five. And we both became aware that we no longer had to shout above the cheering. We looked at the crowd. They were almost completely silent. An occasional piggy cough was the only sound competing with the hissing of the slimers. Forty thousand eyes stared at us in disbelief.

"What do you think is going to happen now?" I asked.

"They don't seem too happy, do they?" Jared answered.

The wall behind us rolled upward. Jared and I reached for our pockets, thinking that maybe another pair of Andovians was about to take up the fight. Instead, the two keepers strode into the arena. The guards pushed their freeze pistols into our backs and forced us into the room. Once the wall had re-closed, the Circus Manager appeared. By the scowl on her face, it was easy to see that she'd bet on the other guys.

"You will be sorry that you have harmed such fine creatures!" she spat. "You will die a thousand times for this outrage!"

"No, they won't," called a voice behind her. "The Emperor has other plans for them." Gam joined us. "Well done, you two."

"They have damaged my worms!" The Circus Manager was almost in tears. "I will have them dead."

"No, you won't," Gam declared as he handed

her a blue letter-card. "They belong to His Royal Majesty now. And the Emperor wants me to take care of them. I have to make sure they stay healthy."

He turned to us again as the Circus Manager stomped angrily away. "Just got through," he explained. "I'm glad you were able to save yourselves, so I could save you."

"You know," Jared said. "This is really confusing. I thought you were her slave."

"That was one of the things that wasn't what it seemed." He smiled.

"Does this mean we're free?" I questioned.

"I'll explain everything," he told us. "First, I should introduce myself. The real me."

Jared and I looked at each other, completely puzzled.

Gam grabbed the skin around his neck and slowly began to peel off his flesh. Of course, it wasn't his skin; it was a mask. When he removed it from the top of his head we were face to face with another bald-headed Freetal.

8.
A Perfect Plan

Gam the Freetal took us by hov-cab to a for-tresslike building about twenty stan-minutes from the Imperial Circus.

"I think you'll find the accommodations a bit better than last night," he said.

Jared and I were directed to separate rooms. Except for the out-of-proportion furniture, my room was similar to an Earth hotel.

"I imagine you want to take a shower," Gam observed as I peeled caked, dry mucus from my arm. "There's a robe behind the washroom door. Leave your clothes in the hallway and I'll have someone pick them up."

After a long shower, I donned the robe and turned on the vid. There was a comedy show about a group of Freetals who were shipwrecked on a tropical island. It was kind of stupid, but for some reason, it reminded me of Earth.

My clothes were returned, cleaned and slime-free, by a young Freetal who regarded me curiously when I opened the door.

A short time after that, Gam and Jared knocked on my door.

"I've ordered some food sent to your room," Gam told me. "I thought it would be more practical to eat here. I promise some of our best food."

They sat at the table, and I chose the more comfortable couch.

"Now you must have a few questions for me," Gam said. "So before we begin, let me tell you that Gam *is* my real Freetal name. The human name, I borrowed from someone I met a few years ago. And I'm very pleased that you managed to beat those slimers. Although I've known you less than a day, I'm already quite fond of you."

Maybe he expected us to say we felt the same way. We didn't feel it, and we didn't say it. He seemed a little disappointed.

Gam folded his stubby fingers on the table. "What would you like to know first?"

"Where are we?" Jared beat me to the question.

"The Department of Special Services," Gam answered. "We just call it the Department. We handle all the special things that the Emperor needs. Things that he doesn't want anyone to know about."

"You're a spy?" I asked.

"I guess you could say that," Gam chuckled. "But I like to think of myself as a little more than that. For instance, I'm a first-class Pretender."

"A what?" Jared and I said together.

"A Pretender, a master of disguise," he explained. "I can transform myself into half the creatures in the galaxy. I was a pretty good human, huh?"

"You had me fooled," Jared told him. "Even now I find it hard to hear your voice coming out of that face . . . I mean, your face. How did you do it? Your arms and legs were longer when you were one of us. And you were skinnier."

"I used extenders to make my arms and legs human size. An extender is something attached to your own feet and hands to change their shape or length. A good Pretender can use them like they were part of his body. To look like you, I wore a bodysuit — made it myself in less than a stan-hour, another skill of a good Pretender. The teeth were a problem. I didn't have time for proper dentures and had to use a set I'd made when I pretended to be a Gormese leaf leaper."

Then he patted his ample stomach. "I wore a girdle to slim me down. It was somewhat uncomfortable."

"Why did you pretend to be one of us in the first place?" Jared asked.

"Right," I said. "What's all this about?"

Before we could hear the answer, there was a soft knock on the door. The Freetal who had returned my clothes entered with a trolley of edibles. As Gam promised, the food was good, all vegetarian — sweetened pastas and spiced leaves and roots.

As we ate our meal, Gam started to tell us what had happened and what was about to happen.

"I pretended to be one of you because I had a hunch," he began. "You see, when those Torkans first signaled that they were bringing in humans to sell to the Circus, I was immediately struck with the idea that you might be the ones I was looking for."

"I don't understand," I said as I chomped some dandelionlike leaves.

"Let me back up a little. When I was young, I was on the Freetal team that met with the United Galaxy Federation to discuss a potential trade treaty. As you may know, those talks got nowhere. The Emperor was, and still is, afraid that joining the United Galaxy would weaken his power in some way. He even threatened war to keep the UGF away."

"The Freetal Empire is a forbidden place to us," I said.

"Exactly," Gam agreed. "Except for the few

smugglers and pirates like the Torkans, we keep to ourselves."

"So how come you know how to speak English?" Jared asked.

"Another skill of mine," Gam bragged. "I can learn another language very quickly — know twelve of them. During those trade talks, I met several humans and managed to learn your main human language, English. I often listen to United Galaxy channels just to keep in practice. My job lets me monitor UGF activities."

"You mean you're spying on us," I said.

"Just curious," he smiled. "Anyway, that's where I met Gambini, the person whose name I borrowed. We became friends during those talks. He gave me a book as a parting gift. It was about the Roman Empire. Sort of came in useful, didn't it?"

"None of this explains why you dressed up as a human," Jared pointed out.

"I'm getting to that. As I said, when I heard the Torkans were bringing you in, I had a hunch. But I needed to be sure. I needed to find out if you'd be able to do the task. So I had to get to know you in a hurry. It made sense that you'd be more at ease with me if you thought I was one of you. That's why I made the bodysuit and pretended. And after a few minutes of talking to you, I knew you were perfect."

"Perfect for what?" I asked.

"The Princess Vinegold." Gam leaned back in his chair.

Jared looked at me and shrugged. "This is getting more confusing all the time," he told Gam.

"It's fairly simple really," Gam said. "Princess Vinegold is the Emperor's only daughter, his pride and joy and heir to the royal throne. A stanyear ago, she was kidnapped by the Emperor's cousin, Rothgar the Terrible. Right now, she's being held captive on the planet Weke. Rothgar wants it for himself. He's pulled out of the Freetal Empire and rules Weke independently. Of course, that didn't go over too well with the Emperor. But Rothgar says that if the Emperor tries to force Weke back into the Empire, he'll kill Vinegold."

"What has this got to do with us?" Jared asked.

"Well," Gam said, "for a long time, several of us in the Department have been toying with a plan to rescue Vinegold. If the Princess were rescued from Weke, the Emperor could send his battlecruisers and clear up the Rothgar problem."

"A plan?" I wondered.

Gam nodded. "We thought, what would happen if we sent a gift to Vinegold, a gift from her Imperial father, the gift of a pet? It would be an exotic pet, something from outside the Freetal

Empire, something that Rothgar had never seen before. It would appear a mere plaything. But, in reality, it would be an intelligent life-form, something that would help Vinegold to escape."

Jared shook his head in confusion. "I still don't get it."

"Maybe I didn't explain it the right way," Gam said. "I want you to go to Weke and rescue the Princess Vinegold."

My mouth suddenly went dry, and I swallowed a mouthful of cheese-like pasta with difficulty.

"Let me get this straight," I said. "Let me see if I heard everything right. You want Jared and me to pretend to be animals that this Princess Vinegold could have as pets."

"Exactly." Gam grinned. "I'm sure that nobody on Weke has ever seen a human before."

"So we go to this planet of Rothgar the Terrible's pretending to be pets for Vinegold," I went on. "But we're really going there to rescue the Princess."

"Right," Gam agreed. "As I said, no one will suspect you of being intelligent life-forms. It's a perfect plan. You'll get close to Vinegold and help her escape."

"Run that by me again," Jared said.

So Gam did. He explained how we were going to be sent to Weke as a gift for the Princess. He'd design bodysuits for us, something that would make us "a little more cuddly." Once there, we'd pose as less intelligent life-forms and we'd be able to free the kidnapped Princess.

When Gam finished, Jared asked, "What if we don't want to do that?"

Gam scratched his wrinkled head. "Well, I don't think you really have all that much choice. The Emperor will return you to Earth only if you rescue his daughter. Why would he save you from the Circus if he thought you would refuse?"

"So if we say we're not going to do it, we get sent back to the worms?" I asked.

"Probably not." Gam shook his head. "The Emperor would be too upset. He'd probably send you to the Royal House of Pain."

"What's the Royal House of Pain? No, don't answer that," I said. "I can probably imagine."

"So how come *you* don't go?" Jared asked. "If you're such a great Pretender, why don't you dress up as something and go rescue Vinegood yourself?"

"Vinegold," Gam corrected. "I couldn't do it. Neither could another Pretender. We'd have to use extenders to change our shape. The security check at the Weke spaceport would start buzzing like a Vandarian clatter-bug when we passed through it. We can get a bodysuit, and maybe a couple of plastic gas pellets, through the check, but not extenders."

"It isn't fair," Jared protested. "If we don't do it, you'll kill us."

"Not me." Gam shook his head quickly. "I told you that I like you. The Emperor would order your execution."

"Wonderful," I grumbled. "Just wonderful."

"So, you'll do it," Gam said. It wasn't a question, just a simple statement. What choice did we have?

"What if Rothgar the Horrible finds out we're faking?" Jared asked.

"Rothgar the Terrible," Gam said.

"Yeah, him," Jared said.

"I imagine he has his own House of Pain."

I put my plate back on the trolley. I wasn't full, but I definitely wasn't hungry anymore.

"We'll start your training first thing in the morning," Gam said. "The Princess has been taught Unnerstan, but it'll be a good idea if you learn a few Freetal words in case there're a few gaps in her vocab. She's only three stan-years old. And you'll have to learn to act like cute pets. That shouldn't take all that long, either. We should have you on Weke in a few days."

Jared tossed his half-full plate back on the trolley.

"Any more questions?" Gam asked.

"Yeah," I said. "What guarantee do we have that you'll send us back to Earth if we manage to rescue Vinegold?"

"You don't have any at all," Gam said seriously. "You'll just have to trust me."

9.
Vinegold Experts

Over the next three days, Gam became our schoolteacher. From Freetal sunrise to sunset, sixteen stan-hours, we practiced to become pets of Princess Vinegold.

Gam had decided that we should act like Earth monkeys. "Your body shape is close enough, and you've seen enough vids of them, so you should be able to do a fairly good monkey, right?" he reasoned.

"Reeann can do a great monkey," Jared volunteered. "She's a natural at it."

That earned my friend a solid punch in the arm.

"Hey," he complained. "That's going to be a bruise."

"You deserve it," I said.

So we acted like monkeys, squatting instead of sitting, acting semi-intelligently curious, and babbling in "monkey talk." Then we got to do more of the same wearing our bodysuits.

Gam had designed two loose-fitting outfits that left our hands and heads uncovered. Fluffy plush-toy-like fur covered our bodies.

"You'll be so cute that the Princess will fall in love with you," Gam said.

"I think it's an improvement, Reeann," Jared told me.

I worked on the bruise on his arm.

"It doesn't look realistic," I said. "We don't look like monkeys. We look like a couple of kids dressed for Halloween."

Gam disagreed. "You look great. Remember, you don't have to look like monkeys, just act like them. And keep in mind that nobody on Weke has seen a human before. Your suits will be more than convincing.

"Now I've added a couple of things to the suits you might find useful. They're small and packed in plastic, so you should have no trouble with the security check. If you feel carefully, you'll find flapped pockets on the insides of your elbows. In the left arm there is a plastic gas pellet. If you need it, take it out and throw it. When the plastic cracks, there'll be enough sleep gas released to put a Hilrutian gigantibeast to sleep. Of course, this means that you have to make sure you get away as soon as you throw it."

"What's in the other elbow?" I asked.

"Smoke bomb." He grinned. "Break the plastic and you have lots of black smoke for a couple of stan-minutes."

Becoming make-believe pets was the easiest part of the training. The tough part was trying to learn a few Freetal words so we'd be able to speak to the Princess if the Unnerstan failed. Trying to twist our tongues around the Freetal grunts and grumbles was no easy task.

Despite some early frustration, Gam was moderately satisfied by day three. "It's not good, just fair," he grumbled. "But it'll have to do."

"What's the rush, anyway?" Jared asked. "How come we're cramming this stuff?"

"You have to leave tomorrow," Gam said matter-of-factly. "It's the window of best bet."

"Why?" I wondered. "Surely we could become better pets if we had a couple of weeks."

"Without a doubt," Gam agreed. "But Princess Vinegold's birthday is in two days. It's a natural time for the Emperor to send his daughter a gift. If we send you at another time, Rothgar may become too suspicious."

"Why do I feel like I'm being trained for a suicide mission?" Jared grumbled.

The last part of each day was spent getting to know Vinegold. No detail seemed too small for Gam. He told us everything. We knew her birth weight, her allergies, her favorite food, favorite toys, diaper habits, dislikes — everything. We were informed of her childhood accidents, like the time she got her finger caught in a pneumatic toilet flusher, and the day she ate poison plowar berries and had to have her stomach pumped. Then we had to view hundreds of royal pic-vids of the Princess from babyhood until the time she and her nanny were kidnapped from the palace playground last year. And there were several pic-vids that Rothgar the Terrible had sent from Weke, just to prove to the Emperor that his daughter was still alive.

We were Vinegold experts.

On the last night, the three of us ate supper in Jared's room.

"This is going to work," Gam said to us at one point. "I know it."

"I'm glad you think so," Jared told him. "I've been giving this a great deal of thought, and I fail to see how we're going to get Princess Vinegold away from Rothgar. You haven't given us any idea about that."

"And if we do manage to free her, what are we going to do then?" I added. "We'll just be two monkeys and a Freetal toddler stuck on Weke."

"I didn't want to bother you with those details until you needed to know," Gam said. "I have all that information. As soon as you finish eating, I'll tell you."

Once the trolley was removed, Gam brought in a portable holo. He placed it on the table, turned it on, and a clear 3-D image appeared. It was an aerial shot of a fortified castle, a number of smaller buildings that ringed an acid moat, and a large wooded area.

"This is Rothgar's castle," Gam explained. "That's where the Princess is being held captive."

"It looks like you'd need a fuzz ray to get into that place," I said.

"But you're going to get invited inside, aren't you?" Gam pointed out.

"Exactly where will we find Vinegold?" Jared asked.

"We have no idea." Gam shrugged. "But it's not important. You'll be taken to her."

"But if we don't know where she is, how will we know how to get out?" I reasoned.

Gam shrugged again. "That's your part. You'll have to see what's best."

"I thought you said you were going to give us the details," Jared complained.

"I'm sorry I can't tell you what to do inside," he apologized. "You'll just have to 'play it by ear,' as you say in your language. I'm afraid you'll be on your own inside the palace. But once you get outside, head for this spot." He pointed to a small clearing behind the wooded area. "There will be a shuttle waiting for you."

"How are you going to keep a shuttle a secret? Somebody is going to see it," Jared asked.

"The Emperor is going to send a battlecruiser to shadow us," Gam answered. "It'll arrive a few hours after we arrive and will hide behind Weke's smallest moon. From there, it will send the shuttle by remote control. That forest is Rothgar's private hunting land. Nobody is allowed to go there. And there are no motion detectors in place; Rothgar thinks they upset the animals. If the shuttle flies low, it'll be undetected."

"But there have got to be heat sensors closer to the castle," Jared said.

"Sure there are," Gam agreed. "But they're set up to detect somebody approaching the palace. There won't be anyone to detect because the shuttle will be empty. And you'll be running the other way."

"You make it sound so easy," I said. "But you don't even know if we can get out of the palace."

"I have a feeling." Gam smiled. "You'll get out. And when you get to the shuttle, just press the Alpha key and the computer will take you back to the battlecruiser."

"Hey, Gam — a few stan-seconds ago you said 'after we arrive.' Were you talking about yourself?" Jared asked.

"Sure am." Gam nodded. "A couple of monkeys need someone to take care of them during the flight. I'm going to be the Courier who presents Vinegold's gift. But don't count on me for any help. Rothgar will make me leave right away. I'll be waiting on the battlecruiser."

Gam switched off the holo. "That's it, I guess."

"One last question," I said. "What do you think our chances are? Honestly."

"Not hopeless," he said.

"That good, huh?" I said.

10.
Rothgar the Terrible

The next morning, dressed in our monkey suits, we crawled into a travel cage and Gam took us to a loading dock in the spaceport. He was wearing the uniform of an Imperial Courier — an orange outfit with green stripes around the wrists. There were a few extra wrinkles added to his head to make him appear older and more dignified. Once in the terminal, he gave orders to the two Freetal baggage handlers, telling them how to treat Princess Vinegold's new pets.

We were placed on a conveyor, loaded aboard an Imperial transport, and secured in a pressure hold. We watched the two handlers with interest. (It was allowed — monkeys are known for their curiosity, after all.)

After they'd finished, the Freetal handlers spent a few moments peering at us.

"What are they called?" one of them asked.

The other glanced at the letter-card attached to the cage. "Cuties." He read the Freetal spelling of the English sound. "It says they're called Cuties."

The name was Gam's idea. He liked the English word. It was easily pronounced by Freetals, and he figured it would appeal to a three-year-old princess.

"They look almost intelligent, huh?" the first one remarked.

The second one shook his head. "Hardly. They look sort of stupid to me."

"Urk! Urk!" Jared said in his best monkey-babble.

"No, I think they're smart," the first said. "Look at those faces."

I had the sudden worry that we'd be discovered by this pair of baggage handlers. If we couldn't fool them, how could we fool Rothgar the Terrible?

The second Freetal studied us closely for several seconds. "Naw," he said at last. "They're stupid. They look stupid, and they smell stupid."

"Maybe you're right."

The handlers returned to their work.

The cargo hold was sealed, and I felt the uncomfortable tingling as we went pluslite.

"It's safe to talk now," Jared said.

Gam had asked us to be quiet until the ship went past light speed. "You can never tell who might be wandering by," he'd explained. "But once we're pluslite, the sound distort will stop you from being overheard."

I reached outside and punched the unlock code into the lock. "Don't forget the code," Gam had warned. "You forget this combo and you're stuck in there."

We eased out, loosened the necks of our false suits, and propped ourselves against a pair of cargo containers.

"You don't smell stupid to me," Jared said.

"Thanks. That's the first nice thing you've said to me in a long time."

"You do look stupid, though," he added.

"You just had to say that, didn't you?"

He smiled at me. "You scared?"

"Course. Aren't you?"

"Oh, yeah." He nodded. "But I'm not *scared-scared*."

"*Scared*-scared?"

"You know, I'm not the shaking, panicking kind of scared. It's more like being worried, only different."

"You're making no sense."

"It's like I'm worried about what's happening, but everything seems so unreal that I can't get *scared*-scared about it. It's like I don't really think about being killed if this stupid idea doesn't work. You understand?"

"No," I told him. "I'm definitely more scared than that. But you're right, it does seem unreal. I mean, dressed as monkey-things, halfway between nowhere and a forbidden zone, four days after facing giant Andovian slime worms. It's all — "

"It'll make a good story," Jared interrupted.

"What?"

"When we get back to school. One of our seventh grade teachers will make us write a story on 'How I Spent My Summer Vacation.' It's the same thing every year. This year we'll write 'I Spent My Summer Vacation Kidnapped Into Space.' It's bound to get us a good mark."

"If we get back, nobody will believe us," I said.

"Not *if*, *when* we get back," he said. "And sure, they'll believe us. Who is going to doubt that you're a perfect monkey?"

"Enough of that joke," I warned.

Jared lifted his hand to protect his bruise. "Sorry," he said. "Last time. Honest."

Two stan-hours in a cargo hold of an Imperial cruiser is a long time. There's absolutely nothing to do. We got bored with playing I spy and twenty questions within the first ten minutes. We were almost relieved to crawl back into the cage, reset the lock, and wait for the pluslite tingle to stop. The ship went true-time, shuddered as it entered the atmosphere, and soon we were on the second forbidden planet in less than week.

Minutes after touchdown, we were offloaded into the terminal of the Weke spaceport. We passed through the security checks without problem.

It was obvious that Rothgar the Terrible had a different idea about who he wanted to land on his planet. Unlike the terminal on Freetal itself, with the thousands of aliens hustling about their business, there were only a few piggy faces moving about.

They were definitely Freetals, even more porklike than their cousins on the Emperor's planet. Their legs were squatter, and their noses were peeled backward to expose wide nostrils.

One of the handlers turned to look at us.

"Clurk, clurk," I said.

He walked away from the cage. Except for him, nobody stopped to examine two strange offworld monkeys. The Freetals of Weke didn't seem to be terribly curious creatures.

I glanced at Jared. "How long do you think we're going to be stuck here?"

"Ssshh," he scolded.

Suddenly there was a ruckus at the far end of the terminal. Two Freetals moved quickly toward us. One of them was shouting at the other.

The silent Freetal was dressed in the orange-

and-green uniform of an Imperial Courier. That was Gam. The noisy alien was dressed similar to an old-Earth Viking. He wore black leather trousers and a dark, knitted shirt. Around his shoulders was a robe of gray fur. Gold brooches studded the robe, and several pistols and knives hung from his belt.

They stopped in front of the cage and, immediately, a trio of armed guards appeared behind them. Although we couldn't understand their complete conversation, we did understand enough.

"Please, Prince Rothgar," Gam said. "Please do not act rashly."

So this was Rothgar the Terrible himself? He did look less than pleasant. A large purple scar lined his forehead and he'd had his teeth sharpened to points. I didn't think it was a particularly bright omen to see him so furious.

"I told you, it's *King* Rothgar!" the ruler spat. Then he pounded his fist against the side of the cage. Jared and I jumped with surprise and then did our part by overacting our distress.

Gam came over and made as if he were trying to calm us down. "Don't do that again," he said to Rothgar. "You don't want to harm such valuable creatures."

Rothgar's nostrils flared. "You foul worm. How

dare you speak to the ruler of this planet in such a way?"

I was surprised that Gam didn't back down. "May I remind His Highness that I am a Courier of the Imperial Court, and as such I speak for the Emperor himself."

"The Emperor has no special privileges on Weke," Rothgar growled.

"But as a powerful ruler who is, at least, your equal, he is worth more respect than you are showing," Gam said.

"Do you insult me, Courier?" Rothgar demanded.

"Certainly not, Your Majesty. I'm merely trying to point out that this is a sensitive matter, and your decision should be well-thought-out."

Rothgar pointed a stubby finger at us. "I consider it an insult for my cousin to send his daughter a birthday gift without first asking my permission."

"Is it an insult for a lonely father to send his only daughter a token of his love?" Gam suggested.

"I will determine who sends the Princess presents."

"But surely the Emperor can send a birthday gift to whomever he chooses?" Gam suggested.

"You are playing political games with me, Courier," Rothgar replied. "We all know the situation here. Vinegold is my guest until the Emperor formally decides that Weke is my world. When he does that, she is free to do as the Emperor wishes. But right now she is under my supervision, and I will decide everything that affects her. Is that clear?"

"I will tell your words to the Emperor," Gam said.

"Good." Rothgar made a savage grin. "And give him this message as well." He moved aside and addressed the guards. "Kill these animals," he ordered.

The guards drew their freeze pistols and pointed them at us.

11.
A Pair of Cuties

D on't!" Gam moved in front of us. "Wait!"
The guards didn't lower their freeze pistols.

Neither Jared nor I moved. In fact, we didn't even breathe. I fought the urge to throw my hands over my face and cry out.

"If you stay there, then I will let my guards fire through you," Rothgar warned. "I grow tired of you, anyway. You remind me of my cousin, and that upsets me."

"May I speak to you honestly?" Gam said. "May I speak as one person to another and not as a Courier to a King?"

"What is this trick?"

"It's not a trick," Gam explained. "I speak only truth."

"Then speak fast, scum," Rothgar said. "I am a busy person."

"My master, your cousin, has sent these animals as more than a gift to the Princess."

Was Gam going to tell Rothgar the truth to save his own life, I wondered?

"Killing these animals may bring the Emperor's battlecruisers to destroy you," he went on.

"You are insane, Courier," Rothgar said. "How can two ugly animals do that?"

"It is a feeling I have, Your Highness. Vinegold has been your prisoner for almost a stan-year now. And the Princess is the only thing that prevents the Emperor from sending his battlecruisers."

"Get to the point, Courier," Rothgar snarled.

"Yes, sire." Gam nodded. "In the royal court, there are many advisors who are telling the Emperor to consider the Princess as already dead. And I sense that the Emperor is starting to listen to their words."

"I know my cousin better than that," Rothgar said. "I know that he loves the royal brat."

"That is true, but the advisors say that you will never let her go."

"When the Emperor makes a formal decree that I rule Weke, he will have his daughter back," Rothgar stated.

"But you know that he will never do that," Gam pointed out. "If he lets Weke separate from the Empire, then other planets may copy your example. It might mean the end of the Freetal Empire."

Rothgar the Terrible pointed at us again. "What

does this have to do with these animals?"

"The thing that you have in your favor is the deep love he feels for his daughter. If you let her receive his gift, it will keep that link. The bond will remain strong. But if you kill the animals, it will make the Emperor feel more distant from his daughter. Perhaps too distant. Perhaps the words of the advisors will make sense to him."

Rothgar bared his pointed teeth and made a long, angry hiss. A spray of spit sailed into Gam's face.

Gam wiped his face with his hand. "If you give Vinegold her birthday gift, it will show that you care very much for her well-being," he concluded. "It will show the Emperor that you do hope to return her one day — that maybe there is a way to bring the Princess back home and also give you what you desire."

"I find this hard to believe, Courier," Rothgar said. "I do not believe a birthday gift means so much."

"We are talking about the fate of the whole Empire, Your Highness. The Emperor may find politics force him to abandon his family. Trust my logic on this matter."

"I will think on it," Rothgar announced. He turned to the guards. "Lower your weapons. And take these animals to the Princess."

"Thank you, sire." Gam handed an info-card to

Rothgar. "This is the code to the lock. These animals will be fine pets. They are most tame, housetrained, and can be released from the cage without worry."

"You have not convinced me, Courier," Rothgar grunted. "Perhaps I will let Vinegold have them for a few days and then kill them. Now, you get back on board your ship and get off my planet."

"Yes, sire." Gam bowed again.

Rothgar spun around and stomped away. Two of the guards followed him. The other guard called for the handlers.

Gam leaned close to us. "Good luck," he whispered.

We were transported to Rothgar's castle in the back of an open shuttle truck. This part of Weke was deep in winter, and the bitter wind cut through our fake suits. By the time we crossed the bridge over the acid moat, we were both shivering violently.

As the metal gates closed behind us, I glanced up at the high stone walls. Laser relays were mounted across the top. Anyone trying to climb over would be cut into little slivers. I wondered if and how we were going to get out of this fortress alive.

A pathway had been shoveled in the snow to a wide utility door and several Freetal servants carried us into the castle. They complained about the cold and the weight of the cage. But, except for one comment about how we'd taste in a stew, they displayed the same disinterest as their fellows at the spaceport.

We were placed on an elevator and taken to a large, and fortunately well-heated, room. The carpet was covered by a mess of Freetal toys. There were little piggy dolls, vehicles, and books. In one corner was a play model of a Freetal kitchen, and in the opposite corner was a computer and four holo-games. Little Vinegold sure had enough to keep her amused.

As the servants were leaving, Vinegold entered, dressed in a yellow woollike robe. We recognized the Princess's large, sour-faced Freetal escort as her nanny. Gam had told us that he suspected she had been part of the kidnap plot.

Vinegold looked healthy. She'd put on weight since the last pics we'd seen. But seeing her in person made me realize how young she was. She wasn't a child; she was just a toddler. How were we going to get her to escape with us?

She edged toward us sheepishly, giggling in a little kid way.

"Clurk, glurk," I said.

"Ur, ah, ahah, ah," Jared added.

She giggled louder.

"They funny," she said in Freetal. We couldn't

understand all the conversation between Vinegold and her nanny, but, once again, we could figure out enough to know what was going on.

"Urg, urk," I continued.

She jumped into the air. "Like them!" she shouted.

The nanny wrinkled her nose. "They're disgusting."

Vinegold ran over to us, thrust her hand into our cage, and batted me on the nose.

The nanny moved quickly to snatch the royal arm away. "Careful," she warned. "They might bite."

My eyes were watering, and I had to blink tears away. The Princess wasn't the one who needed protecting.

She put her other hand into the cage and petted Jared's head. "Urka, urka," he cooed.

Vinegold started laughing again. "What they called?" she asked.

The nanny read the card on our cage. "Cuties," she said. "A pair of Cuties."

"Want them out of cage," the Princess ordered.

"No," the nanny said. "Absolutely not. You don't know what they'll do."

"Want them out!" the Princess screamed and stomped her feet. "Want them out now!"

"Stop that," the nanny said. "Stop that or I'll make Uncle Rothgar take them away."

Vinegold let fly a horrendous, ear-stabbing scream and fell face-first onto the floor. She flailed her arms and legs and pounded the carpet. It was the best tantrum I'd ever seen.

"Stop it!" This time it sounded more like a request.

"Arrrggghhh!" the Princess responded.

"Stop it." Now it was definitely a plea.

Jared and I grabbed the bars and watched the incredible performance.

"Arrrrrrrggggggghhhhhh!"

"All right," the nurse said. "We'll talk to Uncle."

The little darling stopped instantly. "Want them out *fast*."

The nanny nodded. "We'll go ask Uncle."

"You go. Me stay here."

The nanny shook her head. "I don't think that's wise."

Once again, the Princess let fly an ear-numbing scream.

"All right, all right," the nanny conceded. "But I want you to promise not to put your hands into the cage."

"I promise," Vinegold said.

"And no mischief."

"I promise," she repeated.

I wouldn't trust her, I thought.

The nurse left to seek Rothgar the Terrible's

permission to open our cage. I wasn't sure how long that would take, but it seemed to me that this could be our only chance to be alone with Vinegold.

Vinegold broke her promise and started petting Jared again. "I'm going to call you Moonbeam," she said. Then she pointed at me. "And I'm going to call you Funny Face."

Funny Face?

Jared winked at me.

"Hello, Vinegold," I said in Unnerstan. "How are you?"

The Princess scrunched up her face. "Funny Face talk? Pets not s'posed to talk," she replied in fairly good Unnerstan.

"We're special pets," Jared said.

"Moonbeam talk, too?" she puzzled.

"We're magic pets," I explained.

Vinegold shook her head. "No such thing as magic. Uncle Rothgar says there's no magic."

"Uncle is wrong," I told her, trying to put as much tenderness into my voice as I could. "If we weren't magic, how could we talk?"

She thought about that for a minute. "Maybe you right. How could Funny Face talk if there was no magic? Funny Face looks too stupid to talk."

"Hey . . ." I began.

Jared interrupted me. "Vinegold, we *are* magic

94

and we've come to take you back to your daddy."

"Don't want to go," the Princess declared. "Uncle Rothgar says that Daddy doesn't love me. He said that Daddy would make me live in a *garbage tank*."

She said *garbage tank* in Freetal, and I had no idea what she was talking about. But I did notice that the Princess held her nose when she said it.

"Your uncle is wrong, Vinegold," I explained. "Your Daddy loves you very much. He loves you so much that he's sent two magic Cuties to bring you home."

"Don't want to go," the Princess repeated.

"But Vinegold — " Jared stopped when the door opened.

The nanny entered the room and glanced around suspiciously.

"I thought I heard other voices in here," she said.

" 'Bout time you got back," Vinegold said crossly. "Open up the cage."

The nanny was still looking around the room.

"I talk to Cuties," Vinegold said impatiently. "Open the cage."

The nanny came closer, removed the info-card from her pocket, and squinted to read the numbers on the lock. "Your uncle says it's all right to let them out of their cage, but they have to stay in the playroom."

"Hurry up!" Vinegold yelled.

The nanny punched the code into the lock, and the door swung slowly open. Jared and I crawled out of the cage cautiously. Vinegold giggled and began to run around us. She started picking up her toys and handing them to us to examine.

And we got into the spirit of the game. We started hopping and gurgling and pretending we were having a simply marvelous time.

"This fun!" Vinegold declared. "Hey, Funny Face, catch this!" One of her dolls bounced off the side of my head.

That caused a laughing fit that lasted for a stan-minute. When she recovered, the Princess waddled over to Jared.

"Give me hug, Moonbeam," she said and she reached for him.

Her hand grabbed the fake fur on his shoulder. She gave him a yank, trying to pull him toward her. But Jared didn't move; the bodysuit did. The fastener around his neck opened. The fake-fur slipped off his shoulder.

"I broke Moonbeam," the Princess said.

The nanny stared at the open suit. "Oh, my!" she gasped as she grabbed Vinegold. "We've got to tell Uncle Rothgar about this. We've got to tell him right away!"

12.
This Is Fun

Jared grabbed a toy shuttle-truck, stood up quickly, and bashed it on the nanny's head. Her eyes bulged with surprise, then closed in unconsciousness. She crumpled to the carpet.

"How come you hit nanny with truck?" Vinegold wondered.

Jared refastened his suit and looked at me. "It was the only thing I could think of. We couldn't let her tell Rothgar, could we?"

I scrambled over and checked the knocked-out nanny.

"I didn't want to hurt her. I just wanted to slow her down for a while," Jared said.

"Well, she's pretty slow now," I told him. "I think she's going to have a decent bump on her head."

"But she's okay?" he asked.

"I think so. She's breathing, anyway."

"How come Moonbeam hit nanny?" Vinegold repeated.

"Nanny was going to do a bad thing," I explained.

"Let's get out of here before she wakes up," Jared suggested.

I nodded and rubbed Vinegold's bald head. "We have to go now, honey. We have to go to Daddy."

She shook her head. "Told you, I don't want to go."

"I know you did," I said. "But I also know that you'll like it where we're going. It'll be warm. You'll have other children to play with, and you'll find that your Daddy loves you very much."

The nanny started moaning.

"Come on, Reeann," Jared said. "We have to go."

"Look, Vinegold," I said. "If I'm not telling the truth, then you can come back here anytime you want."

"Can come back?"

"Sure, we're magic Cuties."

"Can just look, then come back?" she wondered.

"Just take a look," I coaxed.

"All right," she agreed. "You show me."

The nanny moaned again.

Jared opened the door, peered out, and slipped into the hallway. I took Vinegold's hand and followed him.

"Left or right?" Jared asked.

I shrugged. "How do we get out, Vinegold?"

It was obvious from the Princess's blank look that she didn't understand me.

"Outside," I said in Freetal. "How do we get outside of the castle?"

"Don't know," she replied. "Don't know from here. Know from my bedroom."

"Where's that?" Jared asked.

The Princess looked one way and then the other. "Don't know from here."

"How can you not know which way your room is?" Jared snapped.

"Why Moonbeam mad?" she asked. "Is Moonbeam going to hit me on the head like nanny?"

"Moonbeam isn't angry. He just wants to get outside the castle in a hurry," I said soothingly.

Then I glared at Jared. "Don't scare her," I said in English.

"Why don't you use magic?" the Princess asked. "Why don't you just make us be outside?"

"Our magic doesn't work that way," I told her. "Where are the stairs?"

She pointed left. "This way." Then she looked to the right and reconsidered. "I think."

"Let's go," Jared said as he chose Vinegold's first choice.

The playroom hallway joined a larger corridor. Again Vinegold pointed to the left, and we passed several doors marked with Freetal lettering. Although we'd learned a few words of Freetal, we had no idea how to read the alien alphabet.

"Do you know what these signs say?" I asked the Princess.

She shook her head.

The corridor ended at a wide metal door. A large push-bar stretched across its width.

"This looks like the right one," Jared said. "Is this the stairs, Vinegold?"

"Not sure," she said.

"We have no choice," Jared pointed out. "We can't keep walking the hallways."

I nodded in agreement, and Jared eased the push-bar. As soon as the bolt was released, the door swung open automatically. We stared into a noisy dining room.

"Oh, no," I mumbled.

In the center of the room was a long wooden table covered with multicolored foodstuffs. Around the table were ten chairs made of the same wood. Every seat was occupied by a Freetal. At the head of the table, dressed in his Vikinglike splendor, was Rothgar the Terrible himself.

It took a few seconds for the diners to realize that we were standing in the open doorway. The volume of chatter dropped lower and lower until it was replaced by silence. Twenty piggy eyes studied us.

Rothgar rose from his seat. "Vinegold, what are you doing here? Where is your nanny? I gave her orders not to let those animals out of your play-room."

"They're magic Cuties, Uncle Rothgar." The Princess beamed. "They're going to take me to see Daddy."

There were a few gasps followed by more silence.

"Clurk, clurk," I said feebly.

Rothgar stood up, hurled his chair backward, and reached for his freeze pistol. "I should have known not to trust that scum of a Courier!"

"Elbow!" I shouted.

Jared shared my thoughts of self-defense. We both reached for the secret flap and ripped the plastic pellets from the inside of our elbows. We whipped them into the room. Mine cracked on the table, and Jared's shattered on the wall behind Rothgar. Instantly the room filled with green mist.

Rothgar's pistol was leveled at my face by the time the gas enveloped him. He coughed twice, appeared to gag, and then his piggy eyes rolled into his piggy head. He fell back into his chair. The other diners collapsed into their meals.

"Great stuff," Jared exclaimed.

"He had the gun pointed at my head! In another second he would have killed me."

The mist seeped toward us, and we backed down the hallway.

"I forgot to ask Gam how long it would knock them out for," Jared said.

"He almost shot me!"

"Stop bragging," he said. "We've got to get away."

"How come Uncle Rothgar wanted to kill you, Funny Face?" Vinegold asked. "That's not nice to kill Funny Face."

"No, it isn't," I agreed. "Uncle Rothgar doesn't understand how good we are."

"How come everybody fall asleep?"

"That's our magic," Jared told her. Then he grabbed at the sleeve of my fake suit to tell me that we had to move again.

We started to jog down the hall. Halfway along, Vinegold stopped. "Wait, Funny Face," she said. "I remember now. This door is stairs."

Jared turned the knob, and we moved onto a dimly lit landing. The door closed with a soft thud.

The walls were stone and cement, the air cool and damp. Our breath clouded around us as Jared led us down the stairs.

I think I expected the stairway to end with a door that opened to the outside, like fire escapes do in Earth buildings. I figured we'd find ourselves in the courtyard. Hopefully the bridge would be down so we could get over the acid moat.

The stairway did end with a doorway, a small

metal one, but it didn't open into the Weke winter. We entered another hallway.

"I think we're underground," Jared observed.

It was a logical guess. The hallway had been tunneled out of solid rock. Water pipes and electric wires ran along the ceiling. We were about to turn around, to climb the stairs to find the ground level, but we heard the sound of a door opening above us. Someone was on the stairway. Suddenly there were many feet shuffling down the stairs.

In all that had happened to us since we met the Torkans that was the first time we really panicked. We didn't know what to do. We had no plan. We just ran down the hall. In our desperation, we opened every metal door we passed.

The first room exhaled moist air at us as the door slid open. A large fossil-fuel furnace radiated heat from its hot box. The second door revealed four large water pumps and a storage tank.

"What we doing?" Vinegold asked.

We heard the stairway door slam and Freetals shouting to each other. Our pursuers were only seconds behind.

We charged blindly through the next door and slammed it shut behind us. There was a bolt lock in the moulding and I slid it into the slot.

"A kitchen," Jared said. "We're in a kitchen."

An elderly female Freetal was the only occupant of the room. She stood over a large kettle that boiled on one of three stoves. At first, her face showed mild surprise. That quickly turned to fear when I picked up a large soup ladle and raised it over my head to threaten her. She ran with remarkable speed through another door next to a refrigeration unit.

A low humming noise filled the room, and we turned to look at the locked door. White veins of frost formed on the inside.

"This is fun," Vinegold said. "Glad I come with you."

We watched the frost veins join together and form a circle. It rapidly increased in size. Whoever was on the other side of the door was aiming a freeze pistol pointblank at the door. The radiation was robbing heat from the metal. In a few moments it would reach absolute zero and become so brittle that a kick would shatter it like glass.

We charged toward the other door. Jared opened it and then closed it quickly. He bolted the door. "More coming that way," he said.

Within seconds, patterns of frost appeared on the second door.

"We're trapped," I said. "They've caught us. We have nowhere to run."

13.
It Smell Bad

Jared's eyes darted around the kitchen. "There's got to be another way. What about the dumbwaiter?"

"The what?" I said.

"The food elevator thing. If the food is cooked here, then they have to get it upstairs. There has to be a dumbwaiter."

He recognized the small trapdoor in the far wall before he finished the sentence. He ran over and pulled it open. "This will work," he said. "We can go up one at a time."

I glanced at the frost circles on the doors. They were thick and steaming, almost ready. Then I noticed that Vinegold had her eyes fixed on a pizza-box-sized hole next to the fridge.

"What's that?" I asked her.

"The *garbage tank*," she answered.

It was the Freetal word she'd said before. The word we didn't understand. The place where, according to Rothgar, her father was going to make her live.

I moved over and stuck my head inside. It was a chute that went down at a slight angle. There was a weak light at the bottom, but I couldn't make out what was down there. Dried food coated the sides. I figured that this was where they threw the kitchen scraps.

"Come on, Reeann! Hurry!" Jared called from the dumbwaiter.

"No," I said. "Let's go down here. They'll never look for us here."

He dashed over, looked inside, and then peeled dried food off the rim. "It's a garbage drop."

"They won't think we've gone down there," I reasoned. "They'll figure the food elevator. And where will that get us? We'll be upstairs."

"I'm not sure. We don't know what's down there."

There was a savage pounding on the first door. The metal under the frost was splitting.

"We don't have any choice. We don't have the time to go upstairs one by one. We go here or we get caught."

"You're right," Jared agreed. "Go in."

I picked up the Princess. She grabbed the fake-fur on my suit. "Don't want to go in the garbage tank," she said.

"It'll be okay." I tried to sound as if I believed what I was saying. "Just hold onto me and it'll be okay."

She whimpered a little as I placed one leg inside the opening. Jared helped boost us through, and we slid down the food-stained chute. We dropped about five meters before landing in chest-deep putrid water. Our speed submerged us for a moment, and we came up sputtering the foul liquid from our mouths. Vinegold grasped me more tightly.

"It's all right," I lied.

A second later, Jared splashed beside us. He surfaced and tried to wipe the stinking fluid from his face. Lumpy water dripped from his hair and his fake-fur.

"It smell bad," Vinegold cried.

We were in a tank about four yards square. The ceiling was low, easily within reach, a low-power brite-strip was placed in the center. The water was thick and syrupy. Vegetable peelings and other food scrapings floated on the surface. Beneath our feet was a thick layer of slime. It oozed and bubbled when we moved. And as the Princess noted, the stench was nauseating.

"Now I know what a garbage tank is," I said.

Through the chute, we could faintly hear the excited shouting of the Freetals. But nobody bothered to look down the chute. I'd been right about that much, anyway. Nobody would think we'd thrown ourselves into this mess. They'd think we used the food elevator.

"Don't speak too loud," Jared warned. "Our voices may carry to the kitchen."

"I want to get out now," Vinegold whispered.

"Me, too," I whispered back. "Let's find the way out." Then I spoke to Jared in English. "There has to be a way out of here besides the chute, doesn't there?"

"I should think so," he said. "This is some kind of fermentation tank. They must throw all their kitchen garbage down here. A castle this big must have a lot of food waste. After a month or so, you have marvelous fertilizer."

"Marvelous?"

"There's a light here," Jared went on. "Which means that someone probably comes in to clean it out. So there has to be a way out."

"Make your magic take us out of here," Vinegold whispered.

"We will, Viney. We will." Then in English to Jared, "I don't see a door or anything."

"Maybe it's under the water. Maybe they drain the stuff and then come in to clean it out. Start walking around and see if you can find the drainage valve with your feet. I'll start feeling the outside of the walls."

I moved, stirring up numerous bubbles from the bottom slime. They drifted lazily to the surface before bursting more stench into the air.

"I feel sick, Funny Face," Vinegold whimpered.

"It's going to be all right."

As I trudged through the mire, Jared examined the wall around the perimeter. The only thing my feet discovered was ooze.

Jared finished before I did. "Nothing," he said. "Let me take her for a while."

"I'm going to hand you to Moonbeam for a few minutes. Is that okay?"

The Princess nodded her bald head.

It was easier to walk through the muck without Vinegold, but I found nothing, either. The only thing I succeeded in doing was stirring up enough bottom stink to make our stomachs heave.

"Maybe we're going to have to climb back up the kitchen chute," Jared said.

"We'd be caught right away," I pointed out.

"I'm open to suggestions," he said.

"Vinegold, do you know what they do with the stuff from the garbage tank?"

I expected her to say she didn't know. Instead she said, "Take it away."

"Take it away? How do they take it away?"

"In big shuttle-truck," she said. "I watched once. Truck with tank on the back."

"Of course!" Jared exclaimed. "We're underground. They wouldn't drain it. They'd suck it out. Just like a septic tank on Earth. They'd bring in a truck and vacuum the whole mess out."

He looked up at the ceiling, handed Vinegold

back to me, and began to walk around the perimeter again. He stopped in the corner opposite to the kitchen chute and studied the roof. Then he reached up, pressed the roof, and a trapdoor swung open.

"Found it," he said. "It's a utility hole. This is where they must drop the suction pipe. It must go to the ground."

I slogged over and stared up the hole. I couldn't see any light above. But in the faint gloom from the brite-strip, I could see footholds carved in the side.

Jared reached up, grabbed the rim, and pulled himself into the hole. Then his arm dropped back into the tank. "Give me Vinegold."

I passed the Princess up and waited until he'd placed her in front of him.

"We'll climb up and then you follow," he instructed.

They vanished into the blackness.

I grabbed the rim and tried to pull myself up. Chin-ups have never been my best exercise, and it took all my strength to get my head level with the opening. I reached for the footholds and slipped.

I fell back into the tank, dunking my head under the water. I splashed to the surface with the horrible taste of rotting vegetables in my mouth. I spit it out, but it didn't stop my stomach from protesting.

"You okay?" Jared asked.

"Course I'm not okay!" I reached up and managed with total effort to pull myself into the utility hole.

Water from Jared's suit and Vinegold's clothes dripped on me as I followed them upwards. Soon, the dim light from the garbage tank was swallowed up by the utility hole. We found the holds by touch alone. We must have climbed about thirty feet before I bumped my head on Jared's feet.

"I'm at the top," he said.

"What's there?" I asked.

"I think it's just a metal cover. I can't feel any bolts or hinges or anything. I think it's just sitting here."

"Is Vinegold okay?"

"She's great, aren't you, Princess?"

"I still scared, Funny Face," she whispered above me.

"It's lifting," Jared grunted. "I'm moving it. . . ."

There was a metallic thunk, followed by a roll of choice English words. "It's too heavy," he complained. "You're going to have to squeeze up beside us and help."

"There're no holds on the other side," I pointed out.

"Come on up, twist around us, keep your foot in the last hold and then hang on to me," he instructed.

That was just as hard to do as it was to say. After a few elbows in each others' faces, the three of us were squeezed in the width of the utility hole. It was such a tight fit that if we let go, I think we would have stayed wedged between the sides.

"Can you feel the cover?" Jared asked.

"Yeah," I told him. "But only with my left hand. My right is squeezed against the wall. I can't use it."

"It might be enough," Jared said.

The metal cover was icy cold and covered with a layer of frost.

"Ready," Jared said. "Push."

It was good luck that it was dark. I'm sure that if Jared had seen my face he would have laughed. I could feel my features knotted in effort. I was squinting, grimacing, and snarling all at the same time. But I wanted to move that cover more than I'd wanted to do anything.

The metal skreaked, budged, and finally began to rise. When the cover cleared the lip, I felt Jared shove it to the left, sliding it to the side. The pale light from the Weke night washed over us.

"Let me move back down so you and Vinegold can get out," I said.

I received another elbow in my face for my good manners. Jared helped Vinegold over the top, and then he scrambled out after her. I wiped my nose and climbed after them.

We found ourselves outside Rothgar's castle, a good fifteen yards from the acid moat. Six inches of snow covered the ground, and light flurries patterned the air. The light from Weke's moons illuminated the thin clouds. I glanced up at the walls. There were no guards to spot us, just the silhouettes of laser relays. The lights from the main gate glowed around the corner to our right. That meant we were on the east side of the castle.

"The forest is that way." I pointed to our left.

We quickly marched toward the safety of the trees. I was a little curious as to why there weren't any guards posted outside the castle — curious, but grateful. But it was only logical. Rothgar would close the main gate and raise the bridge. How could a toddler and two monkey-whatevers get out? Certainly not over the walls — the laser relays made that a suicide route. And jumping from a window meant a swim in the acid moat — another silly action. It was only natural to concentrate the guards inside.

At least, that's what I thought at the time.

14.
Thanks, Kid

There was a slight westerly breeze, and we used it to guide us through the trees. The shuttle would be in the clearing on the far side of the forest. I hoped.

The trees reminded me of Earth oaks, tall with many branches. Naked of their leaves, they let the moonlight filter to the ground.

At first, we tried to let Vinegold walk on her own, but it soon became obvious that tramping through snow with her short legs was too tough a chore. We took turns carrying her.

Our wet suits did little to protect us from the cold. Fortunately the job of marching and carrying Vinegold kept us warm. The Princess wasn't bothered by the freezing temperature. Even wet, her woollike robe offered some protection. And she hugged us tightly, drawing on our warmth.

"We almost at Daddy's?" she asked.

"Almost," I told her. "We're going to take a ride in a spaceship first."

"Good," she said. "I like that."

We startled a couple of sleeping kangaroolike animals as we walked through the forest. I guessed these were the private hunting stock of Rothgar the Terrible.

Although it was only a mile-and-a-half walk, the snow and the Princess turned it into a two-stan-hour journey. We emerged from the trees into the clearing.

"There," I said. "It's over there."

A shuttle was waiting for us as promised. It rested on its landing pods. A light dusting of snow covered the black paint.

Jared put the Princess down. "I had my doubts that we'd find it waiting for us," he confessed. "I didn't think they'd be able to get it in without anyone knowing."

"They didn't," said a voice to our left.

We turned around and found Rothgar pointing a freeze pistol at us. Behind him were three armed guards and the recovered nanny.

"Put your hands up," he ordered. "I don't know if you have any more of that sleeping gas, but I will not take the chance. If you make any move at all, I will kill you here."

Then he started to laugh, low and throaty. "Ah, what wonderful looks on your faces. You are so disappointed to see me."

All of a sudden, I felt very cold and very tired.

We'd been so close. We'd almost succeeded. And now . . . now, there was no escape. Jared and I were prisoners again.

"The Emperor should have known I would find the shuttle," he went on. "It came in low, and I have no radar in this area because of my animals, but I'm not a fool. I do have ion detectors. They sensed the shuttle's exhaust. I would not leave myself open to attack. My cousin should know me better than that."

We still had the smoke pellets tucked in the elbow flaps of our left arms. But how could we use them now? If we grabbed for them, Rothgar and the guards would cut us down.

I tried to tell myself that there was still hope we could get out of this. But it was so final. How could we fight four freeze pistols?

"Once my guards reported that an unmanned shuttle had landed, I knew who was going to use it. And I knew that, even if you got out of my palace, I would just have to wait for you."

"I'm going home, Uncle Rothgar," Vinegold said. "I'm going to see Daddy."

Rothgar made another throaty chuckle. "It was a futile plan. But a bold one, nonetheless." He actually sounded like he was complimenting us. "And you are brave. Going through the garbage tank was a stroke of genius. The utility hole cover was equipped with a sensor, of course. Your footsteps leading into the forest confirmed my thoughts."

I fought back the stinging sensation that was building behind my eyes.

"What are you, anyway?" Rothgar asked.

"They're Cuties," Vinegold volunteered.

"I am anxious to learn more about you before I kill you," he said. "And I will kill you well. You have caused me much trouble. I do not like being gassed. And I was very worried for the dear Princess." Then he laughed again. "Vinegold, come here."

She made a move to go to her uncle and then stopped.

"Come here, child," the nanny ordered.

Vinegold just stared at her.

"Now!" Rothgar shouted.

"These are magic Cuties, Uncle Rothgar. They said I can go where it's warm, and where I can play with friends. They said I can come back if I don't like it. But I want to see."

Then she reached over and threw her arms around my waist. "And I don't want you to kill Funny Face and Moonbeam. I love them."

I rubbed the top of her head. "Thanks, kid," I whispered.

Rothgar growled in frustration and marched toward us. He snatched Vinegold and hoisted her over his shoulder.

"Let me go," she protested. "Told you that I want to go with Cuties!"

"Shut up, brat!" Rothgar snarled.

The cold seeped through the fake-fur, and I began to shiver.

"Take these creatures to the cells," Rothgar ordered his guards. "And do not treat them gently."

"Don't want to go!" Vinegold shouted. She arched her back so that she was staring into Rothgar's face. Then she started to pummel his nose with her hands. "Don't want to go!"

Rothgar tried to twist his face away and stumbled backward. Vinegold landed on his chest, and he groaned in toddler-inflicted pain.

The three guards and the nanny watched the scene with stunned curiosity. That darling little piggy-princess had given us our chance.

"Elbow!" Jared and I said at the same time. We grabbed the pellets from our left arm flaps and pitched them at the guards and the nanny. There were two soft pops, and immediately the area between us and the Freetals was blocked by black, oily smoke.

"Get the shuttle open!" I yelled at Jared.

I ran toward Vinegold and Rothgar the Terrible. He'd thrown her off and was struggling to his hands and knees. I took a flying jump and landed my rear end right in the middle of his back. He smashed flat on his face with a sorry *ooof*.

I glanced at the smoke. There was the sound of hacking and coughing in the middle of the billowing wall. One of the guards appeared from the mess, but he was rubbing his eyes, in too much discomfort to see what was happening.

I snatched the freeze pistol from Rothgar's hand and shoved the barrel against his piggy head.

"I want you to stay where you are," I told him. "I want you sucking snow until you hear the shuttle take off. You understand?"

He didn't say anything.

"I'm going to be watching you the whole time," I went on. "And if I see you move, you're going to be the late Rothgar the Terrible. You understand?"

He still didn't say anything.

I put a little pressure on the barrel. "Understand?" I repeated.

This time he nodded.

I stood up and took Vinegold's hand. The guard was now looking at me through watering eyes. He raised his freeze pistol in our direction, trying to focus on me. I aimed Rothgar's weapon at his knees. The Freetal howled in pain and dropped into the snow.

"Sorry," I said. He'd be all right. I'd shot him for less than a second, just enough for a few blisters.

I picked up the Princess and ran toward the shuttle. Jared had the entry door open and was waving at me.

"Hurry up!" he shouted.

I tripped once, stumbled on my knees for a few seconds, then regained my footing. As soon as I reached the shuttle, I handed Vinegold to Jared's waiting arms. Then I grabbed the handle to pull myself in.

My threat to Rothgar had been a bluff. I knew I wouldn't be watching him. I knew that I'd be running with the Princess, unable to carry out my threat. And I suppose Rothgar knew that as well.

I heard the paint on the left of the doorway bubble and crack as a freeze ray scarred the shuttle's surface. And I heard the fake-fur crackle as its molecules approached absolute zero. Then I felt the burning needles spreading through my tricep.

I yowled in pain and let go of the handle.

"Reeann!" Jared called.

Rothgar had taken the gun from the fallen guard. He was running toward the spaceship at full sprint.

Carefully I raised my right arm and aimed at Rothgar the Terrible's head. I tightened my grip on the trigger.

And I think I would have shot the Freetal ruler

if a fluke accident hadn't turned the whole scene from drama into comedy.

Another of the guards had found his way out of the wall of smoke. Through his blurred eyes, he must have seen Rothgar charging the shuttle. And he must have seen me taking aim at the Terrible's head and decided to help out by aiming his freeze pistol at me. But he certainly was a rotten shot.

Rothgar's eyes opened in shock. He howled, dropped his gun, and grabbed his backside. The guard had scored a perfect bull's-eye.

In stunned disbelief, Rothgar twisted around to see his attacker. The guard's freeze ray had burned a neat hole in the rear end of his leather pants. Old Uncle Rothgar wasn't going to be sitting down to eat for a while.

Jared's hand grabbed my shoulder. "Get in!" he hollered.

He helped me into the shuttle, closed the door, and keyed the Alpha button on the computer. The shuttle rose gracefully from the clearing. It kept a low pattern over the Weke countryside, gained speed gradually, then tipped at a sharp incline, increased speed, and pulled out of the atmosphere.

"How's your arm?" Jared asked.

"You okay, Funny Face?" Vinegold added. "I

didn't think that Uncle Rothgar was mean."

"You should hear what your father tried to do to us in his Circus," I told her as I regarded the Oreo-sized hole in my suit. I gingerly touched the burnt skin.

"Bad?" Jared wondered.

"I don't think so," I told him. "It hurts, so that's a good sign. I don't think there's any third degree burn."

I shuffled in my seat in an attempt to get comfortable. There wasn't any extra room in the shuttle, and our long legs were scrunched in the Freetal-designed seats. Jared lifted Vinegold off his lap and wedged her between us.

"According to the computer, we'll rendezvous with the Emperor's battlecruiser in about fifteen stan-minutes. The Freetals will fix you up," Jared said.

"We're almost home now," I told the Princess.

"What my Daddy do to you?" Vinegold wanted to know.

"Well, it wasn't really your father, but it was his Circus . . ." I began.

After I'd finished telling her about the Andovian slime worms, the little kid seemed genuinely upset. "I'm glad you got out safe," she said.

"Me, too." I kissed her head.

"What's that?" Jared asked. "Next to your monitor?"

I glanced at the computer vid-display in front of me. Taped beneath the controls was a yellow tapedisc. Our names had been penned on the surface. They were written in English.

"What's the note say?" Jared asked.

"It's not a note. It's just our names."

"Gam?"

"Who else knows English within ten thousand light-years of this place?"

I slipped the disc into the console. Gam's voice filled the shuttle. He was speaking softly, almost whispering.

"Reeann, Jared, I have much to say and so little time."

"That's the first time he's ever used our names," I pointed out.

"Sssh."

"I'm making this tape without knowing if you escaped with the Princess. As I said on Freetal, I have great faith in you and think that you will survive. If you don't, then making this tape means I will forfeit my life. But I choose to think that you are listening to me after completing your task."

Gam sighed before continuing. "I waste time. I will get to the point. Cut the computer guidance. You must take manual control of the shuttle. You must not take Vinegold aboard the Imperial battlecruiser. If you do, I think you may be killed."

"Look," Vinegold said as she pointed out the window. "There's other shuttles."

She was wrong. They weren't shuttles. They were Imperial fighters — three on each side. Each one had enough firepower to blow away half a moon.

15.
Is There Any Doubt?

The tapedisc continued to roll.

"This is just my feeling, but I don't think the Emperor will allow you to live," Gam's recorded voice explained. "Even if he doesn't kill you, I'm sure that he will never allow you to return to your home. You see, you are foreign aliens, and you now know that the Freetal Empire is not as strong as it seems from outside. Rothgar is in rebellion and, as I said, other planets may also wish to leave Imperial control.

"It is only logical for the Emperor to believe that you will return to the United Galaxy Federation with this information. And the Emperor is a suspicious man. He will think that certain members of your Federation might support a rebellion against him. He cannot afford that. Rothgar would not need the Princess Vinegold if he had signed a treaty with the UGF and Weke was protected by your battlecruisers. Do you understand?"

"What's he saying?" Vinegold wanted to know.

"He's telling us that your Daddy isn't going to treat us very well. Maybe even kill us," Jared told her.

"Why would Daddy be mean?" she wondered. "How come everyone is mean to you?"

"There is a freeworld just outside our territory called Yugur," Gam continued. "The shuttle has enough fuel for a pluslite trip to that planet. The Freetal Empire has an embassy there. So does the United Galaxy. You must cut the automatic navigation and take manual control of the shuttle. Yugur's sun is Lepto Selby, sector 8, section 45, quadrant 7.8, sub-space R5. I trust that you can reprogram the computer. Good luck, humans. I hope we can meet again as friends."

"No problem," I said as I turned off the automatic navigation. I began to punch the directional information for Yugur into the computer.

"What's going on?" Vinegold asked.

"We have to take a little detour," I said.

"You forgetting about them?" Jared waved at our six armed escorts. "Do you think they're going to let us change course?"

I continued to program a course to planet Yugur. "They're no problem."

The radio crackled. "Wing commander, blue squadron," a Freetal voice introduced itself. "We are your escort to the Imperial battlecruiser. Is there a problem with your guidance system? You are straying from your course."

"We changed our plans," Jared said. "We want to go somewhere else."

The radio link was still open, but there was a moment of silence before the voice replied. "You are ordered to reset the guidance system. You are forbidden to change course."

"We'll give you a call to tell you where you can pick up Vinegold," I said. "Don't worry about her. She'll be fine. We're quite fond of her, actually."

She smiled at me.

"If you do not reset original course immediately, you will be destroyed," the voice threatened.

". . . sub-space R5." I finished inputting the computer. "We're all set," I announced.

"What about their threat?" Jared asked.

"Think about it, Jared." I grinned.

He smiled back. "Let's go visit Yugur."

I took the controls and opened the throttle. The shuttle accelerated rapidly.

Jared pulled the tapedisc from the console and crumpled it. No Freetal was going to find out who had helped us.

"You will be destroyed if you attempt to go pluslite," the voice warned.

"Good-bye," Jared said as we approached light speed. "This is Moonbeam and Funny Face signing off."

The six fighters shadowed us until we went pluslite, and we lost them in the time distortion.

"How come they didn't stop us like they said?" Vinegold asked.

"Because you're with us," I explained. "They can't destroy Moonbeam and Funny Face with you sitting between us, can they?"

It was an uncomfortable three-stan-hour flight in the cramped shuttle, but we landed on Yugur without problem — unless you consider it a problem that Vinegold had to go to the bathroom halfway there, and there was no toilet hose on board.

The Yugurians are a humanoid species, very similar to us. We were a source of great curiosity and ended up telling our story to many, many different officials.

They treated my freeze burn right away. The doctor told me that I'd have a scar, but gene-surgery would remove it. I'm not sure I'll have it done. I'm sort of proud of it.

Vinegold was returned to the Freetal Embassy, and we were handed over to the United Galaxy Federation ambassador, a tall Selgelian. He was so pleased with our celebrity status that he threw two parties in our honor. Then he arranged first-class seats on the weekly Pan-Galaxy Transport back to UGF territory.

We had said a hasty good-bye to the Princess and figured that we'd probably never see her again. It was a surprise when a Freetal official and a Yugurian security agent approached us in the departure lounge of the spaceport.

"Her Imperial Highness requests your presence," the Freetal said.

"Your safety has been guaranteed," the security agent added.

"*Her* Imperial Highness?" Jared said.

"The Princess Vinegold," the Freetal explained.

We were ushered into a private waiting room. The Princess was seated in a chair with five Imperial guards standing around her. She had a curious look when we entered and spent a few moments studying us.

"I been told you don't look the same as before," she said. "I been told that you not Cuties anymore. But you still look all right. You look a lot better, Funny Face."

"I appreciate that," I said.

She pointed at the guards. "These people come from Daddy. They come to take me home."

"That's great," Jared said.

"They said I couldn't say good-bye to you. I tell them I'm Princess, and I can see who I want. Then

I scream and stomp my feet. They change their mind."

"Good for you." I smiled.

"They say you not magic."

I shook my head. "We're not magic."

"Uncle Rothgar was bad, huh? He took me from Daddy. I been told that you came to get me back."

"We didn't volunteer," Jared said.

"What?" Vinegold looked puzzled.

"Nothing," Jared said.

"Now I know why Uncle Rothgar wanted to kill you," she went on. "But I don't know why Daddy was so mean. When I get home, I'm going to talk to him."

The thought of that turned my smile into a grin.

"And I'm going to make him stop that Circus thing he did to you."

"That would be nice," I agreed. Who knew? maybe she'd have an effect on her old man.

One of the guards leaned over and whispered into her ear.

"I got to go now," she said. "There's a spaceship waiting for me. I'm glad I got to see you again. Thank you for helping me."

"You're welcome," I said.

"Maybe you get to visit me one day," she said.

"Maybe," we agreed.

"Good-bye, Vinegold." I bent down and gave her bald, piggy head a last kiss.

Jared did the same thing.

"Hey, Princess," he said. "There's one thing you can do for us when you get home."

"What, Moonbeam?"

"There's somebody who works for your daddy called Gam. Ask your dad to do something nice for him."

"You got it, Moonbeam." She grinned. "Something nice for Gam."

Then she stood up and walked proudly on her stubby legs toward the loading door. We watched the Imperial guards shuffle after her. She was going to do all right for herself. No doubt about it, she was going to be a fine Empress one day.

Once the Pan-Galaxy Transport went pluslite, we were able to use the vid-phones to speak to our families. The ambassador had informed them of our adventure through his courier flight two standays before, but we couldn't talk to them personally until we were in time distortion.

I spent a tearful stan-hour with the faces of my parents and sister crying at me on the monitor. I returned to my first-class seat wiping the wetness from my face.

"How's it going?" Jared asked.

"I hate the tingling," I told him. "I hate flying pluslite."

"I mean with your family," he said.

"Let's just say that we're glad to see each other."

"My parents had a funeral for me," Jared said. "Well, not really a funeral, more like a memorial service. They figured that you and I drifted off an asteroid, and that we were in frozen orbit for the rest of time. That's sort of romantic when you think of it."

"They were just glad to get rid of you," I teased.

Jared raised his fist as if he were going to take a swing at my arm. "I owe you a couple, don't I?"

I held up my hands. "Peace. Let's call it even."

"Okay," he agreed. "As long as you promise that you'll never tell anybody what I told you in the Circus cell that night. You know, about my blanket?"

I crossed my heart. "My lips are sealed. And you promise no monkey jokes?"

He nodded, and we shook on it.

A little Torkan kid wandered in from the economy class cabin and stopped by our seats. He had a hyper-blaster resting on his shoulder. It was pumping out what I supposed was hot stuff on the Torkan hit parade.

The little koala bear stared at us.

"Go away," Jared said in Unnerstan.

"Make me!" The little guy cranked up the volume and gave us a defiant look.

"Do you think that all Torkans are obnoxious?" Jared grumbled.

"Don't worry about it," I said. "I happen to know how to speak to Torkans."

"Since when?"

"Since I was kidnapped into space by a couple of overgrown koala bears."

I leaned over and turned down the volume on the blaster. "Look, kid," I growled. "Get lost OR YOU DIE!"

His mouth dropped open, and he started nodding his head quickly. Then he charged back to economy class.

"See what I mean?" I said.

"Clurk, clurk!" Jared said.

APPLE®PAPERBACKS

Pick an Apple and Polish Off Some Great Reading!

NEW APPLE TITLES

America's Favorite Series

THE BABY-SITTERS CLUB®

by Ann M. Martin

Collect Them All!

The seven girls at Stoneybrook Middle School get into all kinds of adventures...with school, boys, and, of course, baby-sitting!